ASIMOV'S CHOICE:

Black Holes & Bug-Eyed-Monsters

Edited by George H. Scithers

DAVIS PUBLICATIONS, INC.
229 PARK AVENUE SOUTH
NEW YORK, N.Y. 10003

Grateful acknowledgment is hereby made for permission to reprint
the following:
Good-Bye, Robinson Crusoe by John Varley, reprinted by permission of the author.
Machismo on Byronia by Martin Gardner, reprinted by permission
of the author.
Low Grade Ore by Kevin O'Donnell, Jr., reprinted by permission of
the author.
Backspace by F. M. Busby, reprinted by permission of the author.
Perchance to Dream by Sally A. Sellers, reprinted by permission of
the author.
On the Martian Problem by Randall Garrett, reprinted by permission of Tracy E. Blackstone Literary Agency.
The Missing Item by Isaac Asimov, reprinted by permission of the
author.
Home Team Advantage by Jack C. Haldeman II, reprinted by permission of the author.
Air Raid by Herb Boehm, reprinted by permission of the author.
A Simple Outside Job by Robert Lee Hawkins, reprinted by permission of the author.
Time and Hagakure by Steven Utley, reprinted by permission of
the author.
Coming of Age in Henson's Tube by William Jon Watkins, reprinted by permission of the author.
To Sin Against Systems by Garry R. Osgood, reprinted by permission of the author.

CONTENTS

Cover Painting by Frank Kelly Freas
Interior drawings by Rick Sternbach,
Frank Kelly Freas, Alex Schomburg,
Roy G. Krenkel, Don R. Bensen, Freff,
and Vincent Di Fate

FOREWORD
by Isaac Asimov

You are holding here something that is a hybrid; a cross between two closely allied art-forms.

It looks like a paperback, and in form and appearance, it is one. Like a paperback, it carries no date on the cover, it shows up without an imposed regularity, it stays in the bookracks as long as those who own the bookrack wish it to.

Nevertheless, it is not a paperback through and through; it was born out of a magazine. You might almost view it as a reincarnation of a magazine, since all the items you will find between these covers have appeared in *Isaac Asimov's Science Fiction Magazine*.

A magazine, unlike a paperback, appears (ideally) with metronome-like regularity. The reader who becomes used to a certain type of literary fare can count on it. He can know to the exact day when he or she may expect another helping. There is a certain comfort and security in this.

And because a magazine is dated, you can make sure that you don't miss an issue. You can even subscribe and make the non-miss automatic.

Nevertheless, magazines stay on the book-stands and newsstands a limited period of time. If you do miss them, they may be gone forever. Or if you have an issue and lose it, you may not be able to replace it, and a story you have enjoyed may be gone.

This hybrid you now hold is designed to give the reader a second chance. Someone who has missed a particular issue, or lost it, can find it now. He'll have a chance to do so for quite a while, for there is no hard and fast disappearance date.

But then, why the magazine at all? Is regularity so important? Cannot a paperback do the job alone?

No, it can't. A paperback without a tight schedule can afford to wait for "name" authors. It can solicit manuscripts and wait that extra month for them. A magazine cannot do this. With a pitiless schedule to keep to, it must publish the best of what it can get. If the experienced pro cannot get a story to the editor in time, then the good story written by an unknown must go in instead.

In short, the magazine and its regularity is hospitable to new, young writers. An undated paperback collection can wait for the established ones. But the health of a specialized field of literature like science fiction depends on a steady infusion of new blood, and without the magazine science fiction is liable to shrivel.

So we need both, and this hybrid you hold will, we hope, combine the good qualities of both by first, supporting the magazine, and second, giving the reader another chance.

It will have, we hope, what is called "hybrid vigor."

GOOD-BYE, ROBINSON CRUSOE
by John Varley

John Varley wrote all through high school, he tells us, stopped when he got out, and took it up again in 1973. Now, reading, writing, and imagining take up all of his spare time.

It was summer, and Piri was in his second childhood. First, second; who counted? His body was young. He had not felt more alive since his original childhood back in the spring, when the sun drew closer and the air began to melt.

He was spending his time at Rarotonga Reef, in the Pacifica disneyland. Pacifica was still under construction, but Rarotonga had been used by the ecologists as a testing ground for the more ambitious barrier-type reef they were building in the south, just off the "Australian" coast. As a result, it was more firmly established than the other biomes. It was open to visitors, but so far only Piri was there. The "sky" disconcerted everyone else.

Piri didn't mind it. He was equipped with a brand-new toy: a fully operational imagination, a selective sense of wonder that allowed him to blank out those parts of his surroundings that failed to fit with his current fantasy.

He awoke with the tropical sun blinking in his face through the palm fronds. He had built a rude shelter from flotsam and detritus on the beach. It was not to protect him from the elements. The disneyland management had the weather well in hand; he might as well have slept in the open. But castaways *always* build some sort of shelter.

He bounced up with the quick alertness that comes from being young and living close to the center of things, brushed sand from his naked body, and ran for the line of breakers at the bottom of the narrow strip of beach.

His gait was awkward. His feet were twice as long as they should have been, with flexible toes that were webbed into flippers. Dry sand showered around his legs as he ran. He was brown as coffee and cream, and hairless.

Piri dived flat to the water, sliced neatly under a wave, and paddled out to waist-height. He paused there. He held his nose and worked his arms up and down, blowing air through his mouth and swallowing at the same time. What looked like long, hairline scars between his lower ribs came open. Red-orange fringes became visible inside them, and gradually lowered. He was no longer an air-breather.

He dived again, mouth open, and this time he did not come up. His esophagus and trachea closed and a new valve came into operation. It would pass water in only one direction, so his diaphragm now functioned as a pump pulling water through his mouth and forcing it out through the gill-slits. The water flowing through this lower chest area caused his gills to engorge with blood, turning them purplish-red and forcing his lungs to collapse upward into his chest cavity. Bubbles of air trickled out his sides, then stopped. His transition was complete.

The water seemed to grow warmer around him. It had been pleasantly cool; now it seemed no temperature at all. It was the result of his body temperature lowering in response to hormones released by an artificial gland in his cranium. He could not afford to burn energy at the rate he had done in the air; the water was too efficient a coolant for that. All through his body arteries and capillaries were constricting as parts of him stabilized at a lower rate of function.

No naturally evolved mammal had ever made the switch from air to water breathing, and the project had taxed the resources of bio-engineering to its limits. But everything in Piri's body was a living part of him. It had taken two full days to install it all.

He knew nothing of the chemical complexities that kept him alive where he should have died quickly from heat loss or oxygen starvation. He knew only the joy of arrowing along the white sandy bottom. The water was clear, blue-green in the distance.

The bottom kept dropping away from him, until suddenly it reached for the waves. He angled up the wall of the reef until his head broke the surface, climbed up the knobs and ledges until he was standing in the sunlight. He took a deep breath and became an air-breather again.

The change cost him some discomfort. He waited until the dizziness and fit of coughing had passed, shivering a little as his body rapidly underwent a reversal to a warm-blooded economy.

It was time for breakfast.

He spent the morning foraging among the tidepools. There were dozens of plants and animals that he had learned to eat raw. He ate a great deal, storing up energy for the afternoon's expedition on the outer reef.

Piri avoided looking at the sky. He wasn't alarmed by it; it did not disconcert him as it did the others. But he had to preserve the illusion that he was actually on a tropical reef in the Pacific Ocean, a castaway, and not a vacationer in an environment bubble below the surface of Pluto.

Soon he became a fish again, and dived off the sea side of the reef.

The water around the reef was oxygen-rich from the constant wave action. Even here, though, he had to remain in motion to keep enough water flowing past his external gill fringes. But he could move more slowly as he wound his way down into the darker reaches of the sheer reef face. The reds and yellows of his world were swallowed by the blues and greens and purples. It was quiet. There were sounds to hear, but his ears were not adapted to them. He moved slowly through shafts of blue light, keeping up the bare minimum of water flow.

He hesitated at the ten-meter level. He had thought he was going to his Atlantis Grotto to check out his crab farm. Then he wondered if he ought to hunt up Ocho the Octopus instead. For a panicky moment he was afflicted with the bane of childhood: an inability to decide what to do with himself. Or maybe it was worse, he thought. Maybe it was a sign of growing up. The crab farm bored him, or at least it did today.

He waffled back and forth for several minutes, idly

chasing the tiny red fish that flirted with the anemones. He never caught one. This was no good at all. Surely there was an adventure in this silent fairyland. He had to find one.

An adventure found him, instead. Piri saw something swimming out in the open water, almost at the limits of his vision. It was long and pale, an attenuated missile of raw death. His heart squeezed in panic, and he scuttled for a hollow in the reef.

Piri called him the Ghost. He had seen him many times in the open sea. He was eight meters of mouth, belly and tail: hunger personified. There were those who said the great white shark was the most ferocious carnivore that ever lived. Piri believed it.

It didn't matter that the Ghost was completely harmless to him. The Pacifica management did not like having its guests eaten alive. An adult could elect to go into the water with no protection, providing the necessary waivers were on file. Children had to be implanted with an equalizer. Piri had one, somewhere just below the skin of his left wrist. It was a sonic generator, set to emit a sound that would mean terror to any predator in the water.

The Ghost, like all the sharks, barracudas, morays, and other predators in Pacifica, was not like his cousins who swam the seas of Earth. He had been cloned from cells stored in the Biological Library on Luna. The library had been created two hundred years before as an insurance policy against the extinction of a species. Originally, only endangered species were filed, but for years before the Invasion the directors had been trying to get a sample of everything. Then the Invaders had come, and Lunarians were too busy surviving without help from Occupied Earth to worry about the library. But when the time came to build the disneylands, the library had been ready.

By then, biological engineering had advanced to the point where many modifications could be made in genetic structure. Mostly, the disneyland biologists had left nature alone. But they had changed the predators. In the Ghost, the change was a mutated organ attached to the brain that responded with a flood of fear when a supersonic note was sounded.

So why was the Ghost still out there? Piri blinked his nictating membranes, trying to clear his vision. It helped a little. The shape looked a bit different.

Instead of moving back and forth, the tail seemed to be going up and down, perhaps in a scissoring motion. Only one animal swims like that. He gulped down his fear and pushed away from the reef.

But he had waited too long. His fear of the Ghost went beyond simple danger, of which there was none. It was something more basic, an unreasoning reflex that prickled his neck when he saw that long white shape. He couldn't fight it, and didn't want to. But the fear had kept him against the reef, hidden, while the person swam out of reach. He thrashed to catch up, but soon lost track of the moving feet in the gloom.

He had seen gills trailing from the sides of the figure, muted down to a deep blue-black by the depths. He had the impression that it was a woman.

Tongatown was the only human habitation on the island. It housed a crew of maintenance people and their children, about fifty in all, in grass huts patterned after those of South Sea natives. A few of the buildings concealed elevators that went to the underground rooms that would house the tourists when the project was completed. The shacks would then go at a premium rate, and the beaches would be crowded.

Piri walked into the circle of firelight and greeted his friends. Nighttime was party time in Tongatown. With the day's work over, everybody gathered around the fire and roasted a vat-grown goat or lamb. But the real culinary treats were the fresh vegetable dishes. The ecologists were still working out the kinks in the systems, controlling blooms, planting more of failing species. They often produced huge excesses of edibles that would have cost a fortune on the outside. The workers took some of the excess for themselves. It was understood to be a fringe benefit of the job. It was hard enough to find people who could stand to stay under the Pacifica sky.

"Hi, Piri," said a girl. "You meet any pirates today?" It was Harra, who used to be one of Piri's best friends but had seemed increasingly remote over the last year. She was wearing a handmade grass skirt and a lot of flowers, tied into strings that looped around her body. She was fifteen now, and Piri was . . . but who cared? There were no seasons here, only days. Why keep track of time?

Piri didn't know what to say. The two of them had once played together out on the reef. It might be Lost Atlantis, or Submariner, or Reef Pirates; a new plot line and cast of heroes and villains every day. But her question had held such thinly veiled contempt. Didn't she care about the Pirates anymore? What was the matter with her?

She relented when she saw Piri's helpless bewilderment.

"Here, come on and sit down. I saved you a rib." She held out a large chunk of mutton.

Piri took it and sat beside her. He was famished, having had nothing all day since his large breakfast.

"I thought I saw the Ghost today," he said, casually.

Harra shuddered. She wiped her hands on her thighs and looked at him closely.

"Thought? You thought you saw him?" Harra did not care for the Ghost. She had cowered with Piri more than once as they watched him prowl.

"Yep. But I don't think it was really him."

"Where was this?"

"On the sea-side, down about, oh, ten meters. I think it was a woman."

"I don't see how it could be. There's just you and—and Midge and Darvin with—did this woman have an air tank?"

"Nope. Gills. I saw that."

"But there's only you and four others here with gills. And I know where they all were today."

"You used to have gills," he said, with a hint of accusation.

She sighed. "Are we going through that again? I *told* you, I got tired of the flippers. I wanted to move around the *land* some more."

"I can move around the land," he said, darkly.

"All right, all right. You think I deserted you. Did you ever think that you sort of deserted *me*?"

Piri was puzzled by that, but Harra had stood up and walked quickly away. He could follow her, or he could finish his meal. She was right about the flippers. He was no great shakes at chasing anybody.

Piri never worried about anything for too long. He ate, and ate some more, long past the time when everyone else had joined together for the dancing and singing. He usually hung back, anyway. He could sing, but dancing was out of his league.

Just as he was leaning back in the sand, wondering if there were any more corners he could fill up—perhaps another bowl of that shrimp teriyaki?—Harra was back. She sat beside him.

"I talked to my mother about what you said. She said a tourist showed up today. It looks like you were right. It was a woman, and she was amphibious."

Piri felt a vague unease. One tourist was certainly not an invasion, but she could be a harbinger. And amphibious. So far, no one had gone to that expense except for those who planned to live here for a long time. Was his tropical hide-out in danger of being discovered?

"What—what's she doing here?" He absently ate another spoonful of crab cocktail.

"She's looking for *you*," Harra laughed, and elbowed him in the ribs. Then she pounced on him, tickling his ribs until he was howling in helpless glee. He fought back, almost to the point of having the upper hand, but she was bigger and a little more determined. She got him pinned, showering flower petals on him as they struggled. One of the red flowers from her hair was in her eye, and she brushed it away, breathing hard.

"You want to go for a walk on the beach?" she asked.

Harra was fun, but the last few times he'd gone with her she had tried to kiss him. He wasn't ready for that. He was only a kid. He thought she probably had something like that in mind now.

"I'm too full," he said, and it was almost the literal truth. He had stuffed himself disgracefully, and only wanted to curl up in his shack and go to sleep.

Harra said nothing, just sat there getting her breathing under control. At last she nodded, a little jerkily, and got to her feet. Piri wished he could see her face to face. He knew something was wrong. She turned from him and walked away.

Robinson Crusoe was feeling depressed when he got back to his hut. The walk down the beach away from the laughter and singing had been a lonely one. Why had he rejected Harra's offer of companionship? Was it really so bad that she wanted to play new kinds of games?

But no, damn it. She wouldn't play his games, why should he play hers?

After a few minutes of sitting on the beach under the crescent moon, he got into character. Oh, the agony of being a lone castaway, far from the company of fellow creatures, with nothing but faith in God to sustain oneself. Tomorrow he would read from the scriptures, do some more exploring along the rocky north coast, tan some goat hides, maybe get in a little fishing.

With his plans for the morrow laid before him, Piri could go to sleep, wiping away a last tear for distant England.

The ghost woman came to him during the night. She knelt beside him in the sand. She brushed his sandy hair from his eyes and he stirred in his sleep. His feet thrashed.

He was churning through the abyssal deeps, heart hammering, blind to everything but internal terror. Behind him, jaws yawned, almost touching his toes. They closed with a snap.

He sat up woozily. He saw rows of serrated teeth in the line of breakers in front of him. And a tall, white shape in the moonlight dived into a curling breaker and was gone.

"Hello."

Piri sat up with a start. The worst thing about being a child living alone on an island—which, when he thought about it, was the sort of thing every child dreamed of—was not having a warm mother's breast to cry on when you had nightmares. It hadn't affected him much, but when it did, it was pretty bad.

He squinted up into the brightness. She was standing with her head blocking out the sun. He winced, and looked away, down to her feet. They were webbed, with long toes. He looked a little higher. She was nude, and quite beautiful.

"Who . . . ?"

"Are you awake now?" She squatted down beside him. Why had he expected sharp, triangular teeth? His dreams blurred and ran like watercolors in the rain, and he felt much better. She had a nice face. She was smiling at him.

He yawned, and sat up. He was groggy, stiff, and his eyes were coated with sand that didn't come from the beach. It had been an awful night.

"I think so."

"Good. How about some breakfast?" She stood, and went to a basket on the sand.

"I usually—" but his mouth watered when he saw the guavas, melons, kippered herring, and the long brown loaf of bread. She had butter, and some orange marmalade. "Well, maybe just a—" and he had bitten into a succulent slice of melon. But before he could

16

finish it, he was seized by an even stronger urge. He got to his feet and scuttled around the palm tree with the waist-high dark stain and urinated against it.

"Don't tell anybody, huh?" he said, anxiously.

She looked up. "About the tree? Don't worry."

He sat back down and resumed eating the melon. "I could get in a lot of trouble. They gave me a thing and told me to use it."

"It's all right with me," she said, buttering a slice of bread and handing it to him. "Robinson Crusoe never had a portable EcoSan, right?"

Right," he said, not showing his surprise. How did she know *that*?

Piri didn't know quite what to say. Here she was, sharing his morning, as much a fact of life as the beach or the water.

"What's your name?" It was as good a place to start as any.

"Leandra. You can call me Lee."

"I'm—"

"Piri. I heard about you from the people at the party last night. I hope you don't mind me barging in on you like this."

He shrugged, and tried to indicate all the food with the gesture. "Anytime," he said, and laughed. He felt good. It was nice to have someone friendly around after last night. He looked at her again, from a mellower viewpoint.

She was large; quite a bit taller than he was. Her physical age was around thirty, unusually old for a woman. He thought she might be closer to sixty or seventy, but he had nothing to base it on. Piri himself was in his nineties, and who could have known that? She had the slanting eyes that were caused by the addition of transparent eyelids beneath the natural ones. Her hair grew in a narrow band, cropped short, starting between her eyebrows and going over her head to the nape of her neck. Her ears were pinned efficiently against her head, giving her a lean, streamlined look.

"What brings you to Pacifica?" Piri asked.

She reclined on the sand with her hands behind her head, looking very relaxed.

"Claustrophobia." She winked at him. "Not really. I wouldn't survive long in Pluto with *that*." Piri wasn't even sure what it was, but he smiled as if he knew. "Tired of the crowds. I heard that people couldn't enjoy themselves here, what with the sky, but I didn't have any trouble when I visited. So I bought flippers and gills and decided to spend a few weeks skin-diving by myself."

Piri looked at the sky. It was a staggering sight. He'd grown used to it, but knew that it helped not to look up more than he had to.

It was an incomplete illusion, all the more appalling because the half of the sky that had been painted was so very convincing. It looked like it really was the sheer blue of infinity, so when the eye slid over the unpainted overhanging canopy of rock, scarred from blasting, painted with gigantic numbers that were barely visible from twenty kilometers below—one could almost imagine God looking down through the blue opening. It loomed, suspended by nothing, gigatons of rock hanging up there.

Visitors to Pacifica often complained of headaches, usually right on the crown of the head. They were cringing, waiting to get conked.

"Sometimes I wonder how *I* live with it," Piri said.

She laughed. "It's nothing for me. I was a space pilot once."

"Really?" This was catnip to Piri. There's nothing more romantic than a space pilot. He had to hear stories.

The morning hours dwindled as she captured his imagination with a series of tall tales he was sure were mostly fabrication. But who cared? Had he come to the South Seas to hear of the mundane? He felt he had met a kindred spirit, and gradually, fearful of being laughed at, he began to tell her stories of the Reef Pirates, first as wishful wouldn't-it-be-fun-ifs, then more and more seriously as she listened intently. He forgot her age as he began to spin the best of the yarns he and Harra had concocted.

It was a tacit conspiracy between them to be serious about the stories, but that was the whole point. That was the only way it would work, as it had worked with Harra. Somehow, this adult woman was interested in playing the same games he was.

Lying in his bed that night, Piri felt better than he had for months, since before Harra had become so distant. Now that he had a companion, he realized that maintaining a satisfying fantasy world by yourself is hard work. Eventually you need someone to tell the stories to, and to share in the making of them.

They spent the day out on the reef. He showed her his crab farm, and introduced her to Ocho the Octopus, who was his usual shy self. Piri suspected the damn thing only loved him for the treats he brought.

She entered into his games easily and with no trace of adult condescension. He wondered why, and got up the courage to ask her. He was afraid he'd ruin the whole thing, but he had to know. It just wasn't normal.

They were perched on a coral outcropping above the high tide level, catching the last rays of the sun.

"I'm not sure," she said. "I guess you think I'm silly, huh?"

"No, not exactly that. It's just that most adults seem to, well, have more 'important' things on their minds." He put all the contempt he could into the word.

"Maybe I feel the same way you do about it. I'm here to have fun. I sort of feel like I've been re-born into a new element. It's *terrific* down there, you know that. I just didn't feel like I wanted to go into that world alone. I was out there yesterday . . ."

"I thought I saw you."

"Maybe you did. Anyway, I needed a companion,

and I heard about you. It seemed like the polite thing to, well, not to ask you to be my guide, but sort of fit myself into your world. As it were." She frowned, as if she felt she had said too much. "Let's not push it, all right?"

"Oh, sure. It's none of my business."

"I like you, Piri."

"And I like you. I haven't had a friend for . . . too long."

That night at the luau, Lee disappeared. Piri looked for her briefly, but was not really worried. What she did with her nights was her business. He wanted her during the days.

As he was leaving for his home, Harra came up behind him and took his hand. She walked with him for a moment, then could no longer hold it in.

"A word to the wise, old pal," she said. "You'd better stay away from her. She's not going to do you any good."

"What are you talking about? You don't even know her."

"Maybe I do."

"Well, do you or don't you?"

She didn't say anything, then sighed deeply.

"Piri, if you do the smart thing you'll get on that raft of yours and sail to Bikini. Haven't you had any . . . feelings about her? Any premonitions or anything?"

"I don't know what you're talking about," he said, thinking of sharp teeth and white death.

"I think you do. You have to, but you won't face it. That's all I'm saying. It's not my business to meddle in your affairs."

"I'll say it's not. So why did you come out here and put this stuff in my ear?" He stopped, and something tickled at his mind from his past life, some earlier bit of knowledge, carefully suppressed. He was used to it. He knew he was not really a child, and that he had a long life and many experiences stretching out behind him. But he didn't think about it. He hated it when part of his old self started to intrude on him.

"I think you're jealous of her," he said, and knew it was his old, cynical self talking. "She's an adult, Harra. She's no threat to you. And, hell, I know what you've been hinting at these last months. I'm not ready for it, so leave me alone. I'm just a kid."

Her chin came up, and the moonlight flashed in her eyes.

"You idiot. Have you looked at yourself lately? You're not Peter Pan, you know. You're growing up. You're damn near a man."

"That's not true." There was panic in Piri's voice. "I'm only . . . well, I haven't exactly been counting, but I can't be more than nine, ten years—"

"Shit. You're as old as I am, and I've had breasts for two years. But I'm not out to cop you. I can cop with any of seven boys in the village younger than you are, but not you." She threw her hands up in exasperation and stepped back from him. Then, in a sudden fury, she hit him on the chest with the heel of her fist. He fell back, stunned at her violence.

"She *is* an adult," Harra whispered through her teeth. "That's what I came here to warn you against. *I'm* your friend, but you don't know it. Ah, what's the use? I'm fighting against that scared old man in your head, and he won't listen to me. Go ahead, go with her. But she's got some surprises for you."

"What? What surprises?" Piri was shaking, not wanting to listen to her. It was a relief when she spat at his feet, whirled, and ran down the beach.

"Find out for yourself," she yelled back over her shoulder. It sounded like she was crying.

That night, Piri dreamed of white teeth, inches behind him, snapping.

But morning brought Lee, and another fine breakfast in her bulging bag. After a lazy interlude drinking coconut milk, they went to the reef again. The pirates gave them a rough time of it, but they managed to come back alive in time for the nightly gathering.

Harra was there. She was dressed as he had never seen her, in the blue tunic and shorts of the reef maintenance crew. He knew she had taken a job with the disneyland and had been working days with her mother at Bikini, but had not seen her dressed up before. He had just begun to get used to the grass skirt. Not long ago, she had been always nude like him and the other children.

She looked older somehow, and bigger. Maybe it was just the uniform. She still looked like a girl next to Lee. Piri was confused by it, and his thoughts veered protectively away.

Harra did not avoid him, but she was remote in a more important way. It was like she had put on a mask, or possibly taken one off. She carried herself with a dignity that Piri thought was beyond her years.

Lee disappeared just before he was ready to leave. He walked home alone, half hoping Harra would show up so he could apologize for the way he'd talked to her the night before. But she didn't.

He felt the bow-shock of a pressure wave behind him, sensed by some mechanism he was unfamiliar with, like the lateral line of a fish, sensitive to slight changes in the water around him. He knew there was something behind him, closing the gap a little with every wild kick of his flippers.

It was dark. It was always dark when the thing chased him. It was not the wispy, insubstantial thing that darkness was when it settled on the night air, but the primal, eternal night of the depths. He tried to scream with his mouth full of water, but it was a dying gurgle before it passed his lips. The water around him was warm with his blood.

He turned to face it before it was upon him, and saw Harra's face corpse-pale and glowing sickly in the night. But no, it wasn't Harra, it was Lee, and her mouth was far down her body, rimmed with razors, a gaping crescent hole in her chest. He screamed again—

And sat up.

"What? Where are you?"

"I'm right here, it's going to be all right." She held his head as he brought his sobbing under control. She was whispering something but he couldn't understand it, and perhaps wasn't meant to. It was enough. He calmed down quickly, as he always did when he woke from nightmares. If they hung around to haunt him, he never would have stayed by himself for so long.

There was just the moon-lit paleness of her breast before his eyes and the smell of skin and sea water. Her nipple was set. Was it from his tears? No, his lips were tingling and the nipple was hard when it brushed against him. He realized what he had been doing in his sleep.

"You were calling for your mother," she whispered, as though she'd read his mind. "I've heard you shouldn't wake someone from a nightmare. It seemed to calm you down."

"Thanks," he said, quietly. "Thanks for being here, I mean."

She took his cheek in her hand, turned his head slightly, and kissed him. It was not a motherly kiss, and he realized they were not playing the same game. She had changed the rules on him.

"Lee . . ."

"Hush. It's time you learned."

She eased him onto his back, and he was overpowered with *déjà vu*. Her mouth worked downward on his body and it set off chains of associations from his past life. He was familiar with the sensation. It had happened to him often in his second childhood. Something would happen that had happened to him in much the same way before and he would remember a bit of it. He had been seduced by an older woman the first time he was young. She had taught him well, and he remembered it all but didn't want to remember. He was an experienced lover and a child at the same time.

"I'm not old enough," he protested, but she was holding in her hand the evidence that he was old enough, had been old enough for several years. *I'm fourteen years old,* he thought. How could he have kidded himself into thinking he was ten?

"You're a strong young man," she whispered in his ear. "And I'm going to be very disappointed if you keep saying that. You're not a child anymore, Piri. Face it."

"I . . . I guess I'm not."

"Do you know what to do?"

"I think so."

She reclined beside him, drew her legs up. Her body was huge and ghostly and full of limber strength. She would swallow him up, like a shark. The gill slits under her arms opened and shut quickly with her breathing, smelling of salt, iodine, and sweat.

He got on his hands and knees and moved over her.

He woke before she did. The sun was up: another warm, cloudless morning. There would be two thousand more before the first scheduled typhoon.

Piri was a giddy mixture of elation and sadness. It was sad, and he knew it already, that his days of frolicking on the reef were over. He would still go out there, but it would never be the same.

Fourteen years old! Where had the years gone? He was nearly an adult. He moved away from the thought until he found a more acceptable one. He was an adolescent, and a very fortunate one to have been initiated into the mysteries of sex by this strange woman.

He held her as she slept, spooned cozily back to front with his arms around her waist. She had already been playmate, mother, and lover to him. What else did she have in store?

But he didn't care. He was not worried about anything. He already scorned his yesterdays. He was not a boy, but a youth, and he remembered from his other youth what that meant and was excited by it. It was a time of sex, of internal exploration and the exploration of others. He would pursue these new frontiers with the same single-mindedness he had shown on the reef.

He moved against her, slowly, not disturbing her sleep. But she woke as he entered her and turned to give him a sleepy kiss.

They spent the morning involved in each other, until they were content to lie in the sun and soak up heat like glossy reptiles.

"I can hardly believe it," she said. "You've been here for . . . how long? With all these girls and women. And I know at least one of them was interested."

He didn't want to go into it. It was important to him that she not find out he was not really a child. He felt it would change things, and it was not fair. Not fair at all, because it *had* been the first time. In a way he could never have explained to her, last night had been not a rediscovery but an entirely new thing. He had been with many women and it wasn't as if he couldn't remember it. It was all there, and what's more, it showed up in his love-making. He had not been the bumbling teenager, had not needed to be told what to do.

But it was *new*. That old man inside had been a spectator and an invaluable coach, but his hardened viewpoint had not intruded to make last night just another bout. It had been a first time, and the first time is special.

When she persisted in her questions he silenced her in the only way he knew, with a kiss. He could see he had to re-think his relationship to her. She had not asked him questions as a playmate, or a mother. In the one role, she had been seemingly as self-centered as he, interested only in the needs of the moment and her personal needs above all. As a mother, she had offered only wordless comfort in a tight spot.

Now she was his lover. What did lovers do when they weren't making love?

They went for walks on the beach, and on the reef. They swam together, but it was different. They talked a lot.

She soon saw that he didn't want to talk about himself. Except for the odd question here and there that would momentarily confuse him, throw him back to stages of his life he didn't wish to remember, she left his past alone.

They stayed away from the village except to load up on supplies. It was mostly his unspoken wish that kept them away. He had made it clear to everyone in the village many years ago that he was not really a child. It had been necessary to convince them that he could take care of himself on his own, to keep them from being over-protective. They would not spill his secret knowingly, but neither would they lie for him.

So he grew increasingly nervous about his relationship with Lee, founded as it was on a lie. If not a lie, then at least a withholding of the facts. He saw that he must tell her soon, and dreaded it. Part of him was convinced that her attraction to him was based mostly on age difference.

Then she learned he had a raft, and wanted to go on a sailing trip to the edge of the world.

Piri did have a raft, though an old one. They dragged it from the bushes that had grown around it since his last trip and began putting it into shape. Piri was delighted. It was something to do, and it was hard work. They didn't have much time for talking.

It was a simple construction of logs lashed together with rope. Only an insane sailor would put the thing to sea in the Pacific Ocean, but it was safe enough for them. They knew what the weather would be, and the reports were absolutely reliable. And if it came apart, they could swim back.

All the ropes had rotted so badly that even gentle wave action would have quickly pulled it apart. They had to be replaced, a new mast erected, and a new sailcloth installed. Neither of them knew anything about sailing, but Piri knew that the winds blew toward the edge at night and away from it during the day. It was a simple matter of putting up the sail and letting the wind do the navigating.

He checked the schedule to be sure they got there at low tide. It was a moonless night, and he chuckled to himself when he thought of her reaction to the edge of the world. They would sneak up on it in the dark, and the impact would be all the more powerful at sunrise.

But he knew as soon as they were an hour out of Rarotonga that he had made a mistake. There was not much to do there in the night but talk.

"Piri, I've sensed that you don't want to talk about certain things."

"Who? Me?"

She laughed into the empty night. He could barely see her face. The stars were shining brightly, but there were only about a hundred of them installed so far, and all in one part of the sky.

"Yeah, you. You won't talk about yourself. It's like you grew here, sprang up from the ground like a palm tree. And you've got no mother in evidence. You're old enough to have divorced her, but you'd have a guardian somewhere. Someone would be looking after your moral upbringing. The only conclusion is that you don't need an education in moral principles. So you've got a co-pilot."

"Um." She had seen through him. Of course she would have. Why hadn't he realized it?

"So you're a clone. You've had your memories transplanted into a new body, grown from one of your own cells. How old are you? Do you mind my asking?"

"I guess not. Uh . . . what's the date?"

She told him.

"And the year?"

She laughed, but told him that, too.

"Damn. I missed my one-hundredth birthday. Well, so what? It's not important. Lee, does this change anything?"

"Of course not. Listen, I could tell the first time, that first night together. You had that puppy-dog eagerness, all right, but you knew how to handle yourself. Tell me: what's it like?"

"The second childhood, you mean?" He reclined on the gently rocking raft and looked at the little clot of stars. "It's pretty damn great. It's like living in a dream. What kid hasn't wanted to live alone on a tropic isle? I can, because there's an adult in me who'll keep me out of trouble. But for the last seven years I've been a kid. It's you that finally made me grow up a little, maybe sort of late, at that."

"I'm sorry. But it felt like the right time."

"It was. I was afraid of it at first. Listen, I *know* that I'm really a hundred years old, see? I know that all the memories are ready for me when I get to adulthood again. If I think about it, I can remember it all as plain as anything. But I haven't wanted to, and in a way, I still don't want to. The memories are suppressed when you opt for a second childhood instead of being transplanted into another full-grown body."

"I know."

"Do you? Oh, yeah. Intellectually. So did I, but I didn't understand what it meant. It's a nine- or ten-year holiday, not only from your work, but from yourself. When you get into your nineties, you might find that you need it."

She was quiet for a while, lying beside him without touching.

"What about the re-integration? Is that started?"

"I don't know. I've heard it's a little rough. I've been having dreams about something chasing me.

That's probably my former self, right?"

"Could be. What did your older self do?"

He had to think for a moment, but there it was. He'd not thought of it for eight years.

"I was an economic strategist."

Before he knew it, he found himself launching into an explanation of offensive economic policy.

"Did you know that Pluto is in danger of being gutted by currency transfers from the Inner Planets? And you know why? The speed of light, that's why. Time lag. It's killing us. Since the time of the Invasion of Earth it's been humanity's idea—and a good one, I think—that we should stand together. Our whole cultural thrust in that time has been toward a total economic community. But it won't work at Pluto. Independence is in the cards."

She listened as he tried to explain things that only moments before he would have had trouble understanding himself. But it poured out of him like a breached dam, things like inflation multipliers, futures buying on the oxygen and hydrogen exchanges, phantom dollars and their manipulation by central banking interests, and the invisible drain.

"Invisible drain? What's that?"

"It's hard to explain, but it's tied up in the speed of light. It's an economic drain on Pluto that has nothing to do with real goods and services, or labor, or any of the other traditional forces. It has to do with the fact that any information we get from the Inner Planets is already at least nine hours old. In an economy with a stable currency—pegged to gold, for instance, like the classical economies on Earth—it wouldn't matter much, but it would still have an effect. Nine hours can make a difference in prices, in futures, in outlook on the markets. With a floating exchange medium, one where you need the hourly updates on your credit meter to know what your labor input will give you in terms of material output—your personal financial equation, in other words—and the inflation multiplier is something you simply *must* have if the equation is going to balance and you're not going to be wiped out, then time is really of the essence. We operate at a perpetual disadvantage on Pluto in relation to the Inner Planet money markets. For a long time it ran on the order of point three percent leakage due to outdated information. But the inflation multiplier has been accelerating over the years. Some of it's been absorbed by the fact that we've been moving closer to the I.P.; the time lag has been getting shorter as we move into summer. But it can't last. We'll reach the inner point of our orbit and the effects will really start to accelerate. Then it's war."

"War?" She seemed horrified, as well she might be.

"War, in the economic sense. It's a hostile act to renounce a trade agreement, even if it's bleeding you white. It hits every citizen of the Inner Planets in the pocketbook, and we can expect retaliation. We'd be introducing instability by pulling out of the Common Market."

"How bad will it be? Shooting?"

"Not likely. But devastating enough. A depression's no fun. And they'll be planning one for us."

"Isn't there any other course?"

"Someone suggested moving our entire government and all our corporate headquarters to the Inner Planets. It could happen, I guess. But who'd feel like it was ours? We'd be a colony, and that's a worse answer than independence, in the long run."

She was silent for a time, chewing it over. She nodded her head once; he could barely see the movement in the darkness.

"How long until the war?"

He shrugged. "I've been out of touch. I don't know how things have been going. But we can probably take it for another ten years of so. Then we'll have to get out. I'd stock up on real wealth if I were you. Canned goods, air, water, so forth. I don't think it'll get so bad that you'll need those things to stay alive by consuming them. But we may get to a semi-barter situation where they'll be the only valuable things. Your credit meter'll laugh at you when you punch a purchase order, no matter how much work you've put into it."

The raft bumped. They had arrived at the edge of the world.

They moored the raft to one of the rocks on the wall that rose from the open ocean. They were five kilometers out of Rarotonga. They waited for some light as the sun began to rise, then started up the rock face.

It was rough: blasted out with explosives on this face of the dam. It went up at a thirty degree angle for fifty meters, then was suddenly level and smooth as glass. The top of the dam at the edge of the world had been smoothed by cutting lasers into a vast table top, three hundred kilometers long and four kilometers wide. They left wet footprints on it as they began the long walk to the edge.

They soon lost any meaningful perspective on the thing. They lost sight of the sea-edge, and couldn't see the drop-off until they began to near it. By then, it was full light. Timed just right, they would reach the edge when the sun came up and they'd really have something to see.

A hundred meters from the edge when she could see over it a little, Lee began to unconsciously hang back. Piri didn't prod her. It was not something he could force someone to see. He'd reached this point with others, and had to turn back. Already, the fear of falling was building up. But she came on, to stand beside him at the very lip of the canyon.

Pacifica was being built and filled in three sections. Two were complete, but the third was still being hollowed out and was not yet filled with water except in the deepest trenches. The water was kept out of this section by the dam they were standing on. When it was completed, when all the underwater trenches and mountain ranges and guyots and slopes had been

31

built to specifications, the bottom would be covered with sludge and ooze and the whole wedge-shaped section flooded. The water came from liquid hydrogen and oxygen on the surface, combined with the limitless electricity of fusion powerplants.

"We're doing what the Dutch did on Old Earth, but in reverse," Piri pointed out, but he got no reaction from Lee. She was staring, spellbound, down the sheer face of the dam to apparently bottomless trench below. It was shrouded in mist, but seemed to fall off forever.

"It's eight kilometers deep," Piri told her. "It's not going to be a regular trench when it's finished. It's there to be filled up with the remains of this dam after the place has been flooded." He looked at her face, and didn't bother with more statistics. He let her experience it in her own way.

The only comparable vista on a human-inhabited planet was the Great Rift Valley on Mars. Neither of them had seen it, but it suffered in comparison to this because not all of it could be seen at once. Here, one could see from one side to the other, and from sea level to a distance equivalent to the deepest oceanic trenches on Earth. It simply fell away beneath them and went straight down to nothing. There was a rainbow beneath their feet. Off to the left was a huge waterfall that arced away from the wall in a solid stream. Tons of overflow water went through the wall, to twist, fragment, vaporize and blow away long before it reached the bottom of the trench.

Straight ahead of them and about ten kilometers away was the mountain that would become the Okinawa biome when the pit was filled. Only the tiny, blackened tip of the mountain would show above the water.

Lee stayed and looked at it as long as she could. It became easier the longer one stood there, and yet something about it drove her away. The scale was too big, there was no room for humans in that shattered world. Long before noon, they turned and started the long walk back to the raft.

She was silent as they boarded and set sail for the return trip. The winds were blowing fitfully, barely billowing the sail. It would be another hour before they blew very strongly. They were still in sight of the dam wall.

They sat on the raft, not looking at each other.

"Piri, thanks for bringing me here."

"You're welcome. You don't have to talk about it."

"All right. But there's something else I have to talk about. I . . . I don't know where to begin, really."

Piri stirred uneasily. The earlier discussion about economics had disturbed him. It was part of his past life, a part that he had not been ready to return to. He was full of confusion. Thoughts that had no place out here in the concrete world of wind and water were roiling through his brain. Someone was calling to him, someone he knew but didn't want to see right then.

"Yeah? What is it you want to talk about?"

"It's about—" she stopped, seemed to think it over. "Never mind. It's not time yet." She moved close and touched him. But he was not interested. He made it known in a few minutes, and she moved to the other side of the raft.

He lay back, essentially alone with his troubled thoughts. The wind gusted, then settled down. He saw a flying fish leap, almost passing over the raft. There was a piece of the sky falling through the air. It twisted and turned like a feather, a tiny speck of sky that was blue on one side and brown on the other. He could see the hole in the sky where it had been knocked loose.

It must be two or three kilometers away. No, wait, that wasn't right. The top of the sky was twenty kilometers up, and it looked like it was falling from the center. How far away were they from the center of Pacifica? A hundred kilometers?

A piece of the sky?

He got to his feet, nearly capsizing the raft.

"What's the matter?"

It was *big*. It looked large even from this far away. It was the dreamy tumbling motion that had deceived him.

"The sky is . . ." he choked on it, and almost laughed. But this was not time to feel silly about it. "The sky is falling, Lee." How long? He watched it, his mind full of numbers. Terminal velocity from that high up, assuming it was heavy enough to punch right through the atmosphere . . . over six hundred meters per second. Time to fall, seventy seconds. Thirty of those must already have gone by.

Lee was shading her eyes as she followed his gaze. She still thought it was a joke. The chunk of sky began to glow red as the atmosphere got thicker.

"Hey, it really is falling," she said. "Look at that."

"It's big. Maybe one or two kilometers across. It's going to make quite a splash, I'll bet."

They watched it descend. Soon it disappeared over the horizon, picking up speed. They waited, but the show seemed to be over. Why was he still uneasy?

"How many tons in a two-kilometer chunk of rock, I wonder?" Lee mused. She didn't look too happy, either. But they sat back down on the raft, still looking in the direction where the thing had sunk into the sea.

Then they were surrounded by flying fish, and the water looked crazy. The fish were panicked. As soon as they hit they leaped from the water again. Piri felt rather than saw something pass beneath them. And then, very gradually, a roar built up, a deep bass rumble that soon threatened to turn his bones to powder. It picked him up and shook him, and left him limp on his knees. He was stunned, unable to think clearly. His eyes were still fixed on the horizon, and he saw a white fan rising in the distance in silent majesty. It was the spray from the impact, and it was still going up.

"Look up there," Lee said, when she got her voice back. She seemed as confused as he. He looked where she pointed and saw a twisted line crawling across the blue sky. At first he thought it was the end of his life, because it appeared that the whole overhanging dome was fractured and about to fall in on them. But then he saw it was one of the tracks that the sun ran on, pulled free by the rock that had fallen, twisted into a snake of tortured metal.

"The dam!" he yelled. "The dam! The water here isn't that deep. There'll be a wave coming, Lee, a big wave. It'll pile up here."

"Piri, the shadows are moving."

"Huh?"

Surprise was piling on surprise too fast for him to cope with it. But she was right. The shadows were moving. But *why?*

Then he saw it. The sun was setting, but not by following the tracks that led to the concealed opening in the west. It was falling through the air, having been shaken loose by the rock.

Lee had figured it out, too.

"What is that thing?" she asked. "I mean, how big is it?"

"Not too big, I heard. Big enough, but not nearly the size of that chunk that fell. It's some kind of fusion generator. I don't know what'll happen when it hits the water."

They were paralyzed. They knew there was something they should do, but too many things were happening. There was not time to think it out.

"Dive!" Lee yelled. "Dive into the water!"

"What?"

"We have to dive and swim away from the dam, and down as far as we can go. The wave will pass over us, won't it?"

"I don't know."

"It's all we can do."

So they dived. Piri felt his gills come into action, then he was swimming down at an angle toward the

35

dark-shrouded bottom. Lee was off to his left, swimming as hard as she could. And with no sunset, no warning, it got black as pitch. The sun had hit the water.

He had no idea how long he had been swimming when he suddenly felt himself pulled upward. Floating in the water, weightless, he was not well equipped to feel accelerations. But he did feel it, like a rapidly rising elevator. It was accompanied by pressure waves that threatened to burst his eardrums. He kicked and clawed his way downward, not even knowing if he was headed in the right direction. Then he was falling again.

He kept swimming, all alone in the dark. Another wave passed, lifted him, let him down again. A few minutes later, another one, seeming to come from the other direction. He was hopelessly confused. He suddenly felt he was swimming the wrong way. He stopped, not knowing what to do. Was he pointed in the right direction? He had no way to tell.

He stopped paddling and tried to orient himself. It was useless. He felt surges, and was sure he was being tumbled and buffeted.

Then his skin was tingling with the sensation of a million bubbles crawling over him. It gave him a handle on the situation. The bubbles would be going up, wouldn't they? And they were traveling over his body from belly to back. So down was *that* way.

But he didn't have time to make use of the information. He hit something hard with his hip, wrenched his back as his body tried to tumble over in the foam and water, then was sliding along a smooth surface. It felt like he was going very fast, and he knew where he was and where he was heading and there was nothing he could do about it. The tail of the wave had lifted him clear of the rocky slope of the dam and deposited him on the flat surface. It was now spending itself, sweeping him along to the edge of the world. He turned around, feeling the sliding surface beneath him with his hands, and tried to dig in. It was a nightmare; nothing he did had any effect. Then his head broke free into the air.

He was still sliding, but the huge hump of the wave had dissipated itself and was collapsing quietly into froth and puddles. It drained away with amazing speed. He was left there, alone, cheek pressed lovingly to the cold rock. The darkness was total.

He wasn't about to move. For all he knew, there was an eight-kilometer drop just behind his toes.

Maybe there would be another wave. If so, this one would crash down on him instead of lifting him like a cork in a tempest. It should kill him instantly. He refused to worry about that. All he cared about now was not slipping any further.

The stars had vanished. Power failure? Now they blinked on. He raised his head a little, in time to see a soft, diffused glow in the east. The moon was rising, and it was doing it at breakneck speed. He saw it rotate from a thin crescent configuration to bright fullness in under a minute. Someone was still in charge, and had decided to throw some light on the scene.

He stood, though his knees were weak. Tall fountains of spray far away to his right indicated where the sea was battering at the dam. He was about in the middle of the tabletop, far from either edge. The ocean was whipped up as if by thirty hurricanes, but he was safe from it at this distance unless there were another tsunami yet to come.

The moonlight turned the surface into a silver mirror, littered with flopping fish. He saw another figure get to her feet, and ran in that direction.

The helicopter located them by infrared detector. They had no way of telling how long it had been. The moon was hanging motionless in the center of the sky.

They got into the cabin, shivering.

The helicopter pilot was happy to have found them, but grieved over other lives lost. She said the toll stood at three dead, fifteen missing and presumed dead. Most of these had been working on the reefs. All the land surface of Pacifica had been scoured, but the loss of life had been minimal. Most had had time to get to an elevator and go below or to a helicopter and rise above the devastation.

From what they had been able to find out, heat expansion of the crust had moved farther down into the interior of the planet than had been expected. It was summer on the surface, something it was easy to forget down here. The engineers had been sure that the inner surface of the sky had been stabilized years ago, but a new fault had been opened by the slight temperature rise. She pointed up to where ships were hovering like fireflies next to the sky, playing searchlights on the site of the damage. No one knew yet if Pacifica would have to be abandoned for another twenty years while it stabilized.

She set them down on Rarotonga. The place was a mess. The wave had climbed the bottom rise and crested at the reef, and a churning hell of foam and debris had swept over the island. Little was left standing except the concrete blocks that housed the elevators, scoured of their decorative camouflage.

Piri saw a familiar figure coming toward him through the wreckage that had been a picturesque village. She broke into a run, and nearly bowled him over, laughing and kissing him.

"We were sure you were dead," Harra said, drawing back from him as if to check for cuts and bruises.

"It was a fluke, I guess," he said, still incredulous that he had survived. It had seemed bad enough out there in the open ocean; the extent of the disaster was much more evident on the island. He was badly shaken to see it.

"Lee suggested that we try to dive under the wave. That's what saved us. It just lifted us up, then the last one swept us over the top of the dam and drained away. It dropped us like leaves."

"Well, not quite so tenderly in my case," Lee

pointed out. "It gave me quite a jolt. I think I might have sprained my wrist."

A medic was available. While her wrist was being bandaged, she kept looking at Piri. He didn't like the look.

"There's something I'd intended to talk to you about on the raft, or soon after we got home. There's no point in your staying here any longer anyway, and I don't know where you'd go."

"No!" Harra burst out. "Not yet. Don't tell him anything yet. It's not fair. Stay away from him." She was protecting Piri with her body, from no assault that was apparent to him.

"I just wanted to—"

"No, no. Don't listen to her, Piri. Come with me." She pleaded with the other woman. "Just give me a few hours alone with him, there's some things I never got around to telling him."

Lee looked undecided, and Piri felt mounting rage and frustration. He had known things were going on around him. It was mostly his own fault that he had ignored them, but now he had to know. He pulled his hand free from Harra and faced Lee.

"Tell me."

She looked down at her feet, then back to his eyes.

"I'm not what I seem, Piri. I've been leading you along, trying to make this easier for you. But you still fight me. I don't think there's any way it's going to be easy."

"No!" Harra shouted again.

"What are you?"

"I'm a psychiatrist. I specialize in retrieving people like you, people who are in a mental vacation mode, what you call 'second childhood'. You're aware of all this, on another level, but the child in you has fought it at every stage. The result has been nightmares—probably with me as the focus, whether you admitted it or not."

She grasped both his wrists, one of them awkwardly because of her injury.

"Now listen to me." She spoke in an intense whisper, trying to get it all out before the panic she saw in his face broke free and sent him running. "You came here for a vacation. You were going to stay ten years, growing up and taking it easy. That's all over. The situation that prevailed when you left is now out of date. Things have moved faster than you believed possible. You had expected a ten-year period after your return to get things in order for the coming battles. That time has evaporated. The Common Market of the Inner Planets has fired the first shot. They've instituted a new system of accounting and it's locked into their computers and running. It's aimed right at Pluto, and it's been working for a month now. We cannot continue as an economic partner to the C.M.I.P., because from now on every time we sell or buy or move money the inflationary multiplier is automatically juggled against us. It's all perfectly legal by all existing treaties, and it's necessary to their economy. But it ignores our time-lag disadvantage. We have to consider it as a hostile act, no matter what the intent. You have to come back and direct the way, Mister Finance Minister."

The words shattered what calm Piri had left. He wrenched free of her hands and turned wildly to look all around him. Then he sprinted down the beach. He tripped once over his splay feet, got up without ever slowing, and disappeared.

Harra and Lee stood silently and watched him go.

"You didn't have to be so rough with him," Harra said, but knew it wasn't so. She just hated to see him so confused.

"It's best done quickly when they resist. And he's all right. He'll have a fight with himself, but there's no real doubt of the outcome."

"So the Piri I know will be dead soon?"

Lee put her arm around the younger woman.

"Not at all. It's a re-integration, without a winner or a loser. You'll see." She looked at the tear-streaked face.

"Don't worry. You'll like the older Piri. It won't take him any time at all to realize that he loves you."

He had never been to the reef at night. It was a place of furtive fish, always one step ahead of him as they darted back into their places of concealment. He wondered how long it would be before they ventured out in the long night to come. The sun might not rise for years.

They might never come out. Not realizing the changes in their environment, night fish and day fish would never adjust. Feeding cycles would be disrupted, critical temperatures would go awry, the endless moon and lack of sun would frustrate the internal mechanisms, bred over billions of years, and fish would die. It had to happen.

The ecologists would have quite a job on their hands.

But there was one denizen of the outer reef that would survive for a long time. He would eat anything that moved and quite a few things that didn't, at any time of the day or night. He had no fear, he had no internal clocks dictating to him, no inner pressures to confuse him except the one overriding urge to attack. He would last as long as there was anything alive to eat.

But in what passed for a brain in the white-bottomed torpedo that was the Ghost, a splinter of doubt had lodged. He had no recollection of similar doubts, though there had been some. He was not equipped to remember, only to hunt. So this new thing that swam beside him, and drove his cold brain as near as it could come to the emotion of anger, was a mystery. He tried again and again to attack it, then something would seize him with an emotion he had not felt since he was half a meter long, and fear would drive him away.

Piri swam along beside the faint outline of the shark. There was just enough moonlight for him to see the fish, hovering at the ill-defined limit of his sonic signal. Occasionally, the shape would shudder from head to tail, turn toward him, and grow larger. At these times Piri could see nothing but a gaping jaw. Then it would turn quickly, transfix him with that bottomless pit of an eye, and sweep away.

Piri wished he could laugh at the poor, stupid brute. How could he have feared such a mindless eating machine?

Good-bye, pinbrain. He turned and stroked lazily toward the shore. He knew the shark would turn and follow him, nosing into the interdicted sphere of his transponder, but the thought did not impress him. He was without fear. How could he be afraid, when he had already been swallowed into the belly of his nightmare? The teeth had closed around him, he had awakened, and remembered. And that was the end of his fear.

Good-bye, tropical paradise. You were fun while you lasted. Now I'm a grown-up, and must go off to war.

He didn't relish it. It was a wrench to leave his childhood, though the time had surely been right. Now the responsibilities had descended on him, and he must shoulder them. He thought of Harra.

"Piri," he told himself, "as a teenager, you were just too dumb to live."

Knowing it was the last time, he felt the coolness of the water flowing over his gills. They had served him well, but had no place in his work. There was no place for a fish, and no place for Robinson Crusoe.

Good-bye, gills.

He kicked harder for the shore and came to stand, dripping wet, on the beach. Harra and Lee were there, waiting for him.

MACHISMO ON BYRONIA
by Martin Gardner

This time, Mr. Gardner has provided us a statistics puzzle, a variation of his own on an older theme. This one contains three successive questions, and therefore, three solutions.

Byronia, a small planet that orbits a sun near ours, has a humanoid population similar to our own. The most striking difference is that Byronians come in three sexes. They correspond roughly to what we call male, female, and bisexual.

Because bisexuals have both male and female organs, they can perform as either sex and also bear children. Whenever a "mother" (female or bisexual) gives birth, the probability that the child is male, female, or bisexual is exactly ⅓ for each.

The new Supreme Ruler of Byronia, Norman Machismo, is a virile, hot-tempered male who gained total power by defeating a rebellious army of bisexuals. To solve the "bisexual problem" Machismo has issued the following decree: Every mother on Byronia, as soon as she or it gives birth to a bisexual, is to be rendered incapable of further conception.

Machismo reasoned like this. Some mothers are sure to have two, three, four, or even more heterosexuals before having a bisexual. True, occasionally a mother will have a bisexual first child, but that will be the end of her childbearing so these births will contribute only a small percentage of bisexuals to the population. In this way the proportion of bisexuals in the population will steadily diminish.

Will the Supreme Ruler's plan work? See page 132 for the solution.

LOW GRADE ORE
by Kevin O'Donnell, Jr.

The author was born 26 years ago in Cleveland, Ohio, where he grew up. He spent two years in Korea, one in Hong Kong, and one in Taipei. Like many writers, he's worked at a wide range of jobs: groundskeeping, teaching English, managing a dining hall, and various positions in a hospital. He now lives in New Haven with his wife, Lillian, where he is working on a novel along with his short stories—of which he's sold 19.

45

Nobody knew the teleport's name. Unless she'd come alone, her parents had also disappeared. Repeated appeals through the scratchy loudspeaker system had drawn no one willing to claim knowledge of her, much less a relationship. Perhaps they were peasants, fearful of reprisals if her identity were known.

By 19:49, the Director of the Calcutta Evaluation Center was answering the rapid-fire questions of fifty unruly newsmen. He spoke in English, probably to avoid accusations of regional favoritism. "Yes," he was saying, "we should be able to find it from her computer card, as we did on the three previous occasions, but—" He spread his dusky hands in dismay.

A cameraman from a local station lined his equipment up to frame the Director's pudgy figure with the ever-shifting colors of the Pukcip hologram.

"To the best of our admittedly limited knowledge, the child did present her card; the question now is, where has it gone? You must understand that immediately after she teleported to Pukci, at 13:46, there arose more commotion than the staff could cope with yet—" as the photographer readied his videotape camera, the Director, a political appointee, dried his forehead, "—I assure you, gentlemen, that as soon as conditions permit we shall crosscheck all cards on file quite thoroughly, and—"

A little girl's desperate shriek froze everyone. The audience's attention shifted from the director; he swayed visibly, as though brushed by a gust of wind. The camera whirred while its handler murmured clipped phrases of excitement into its microphone.

Between the straining reporters and the hologram stood the six-year-old whom the Pukcip screening had swallowed. Her hair was gone, shaved to the scalp; her dark skin was streaked and smeared with blood. She was naked except for wires that flapped from her wrists, her ankles, and her knobbly bald head.

They began to mutter. Was this what the Pukcip

did to the children who precipitated out? Slowly, their hostility focused on the intermediary—

The child's second scream was ghastly in its inhumanity. It was the throat-tearing cry of a mortally wounded animal. Staggering towards them, she raised her tiny hands as though to beg their help.

A few in the front shook off their numbness, opened their arms, stepped—

Two Pukcip warriors materialized; the almost-saviors lurched back as if from a gout of flame. Each warrior held a gun in its posterior hands; each trained one stalked eye on the startled newsmen. Their anterior hands reached for the girl. She dodged. They teleported to either side of her. One seized her arms; the other, her legs. The one whose kaleidoscopic carapace was more ornate dipped its eyestalks at the crowd that had begun to press forward. An instant later, all three—warriors and child, aliens and human—had vanished as though they'd never been.

The heavy silence of shock hung over the room for an awful minute, then burst into a monsoon rain of anger. The Director was its center. Bodies shoved; voices shouted. His mouth worked frantically, but futilely, against the frustration that mounted like a storm's static charge.

"Gentlemen, gentlemen, please, this is no—" His fat hands waved in vain. He was the lightning rod; their hatred, a rising surf, needed a rock on which to break. A fist beat against his face, and then another. He gave one strangled cry before his final, fatal inundation.

Even as the white-helmeted police were cracking enough black-haired skulls to disperse the mob, a bruised witness described the cameraman. Through channels hypersensitive to bad publicity flashed the order to suppress the tape.

The station manager surrendered it, though he protested that the government should not obscure the truth, not when a thousand hugely distorted rumors were flickering like cobra tongues through the Calcutta slums.

His superiors, apparently confident that tempers ignited by gossip needed hard fact to sustain their heat, ignored him.

They were wrong.

Calcutta burned.

A step ahead of the flames worked a score of foreign agents, laboring to discover just why the uneasy peace had been shattered. One "cultural attache" after another spoke to the survivors of the press conference; one government after another decided that it had to view the tape.

New Delhi, resisting their demands, insisted that it was a purely internal affair. In private and off the record, its distracted officials promised to distribute the tape once the civil disorders had ended.

Russian and American strategic analysts were skeptical. Oft-declared "states of emergency" had overprotected the Indian government from reality; it could not, they maintained, outlast an actual emergency.

Red phones buzzed; edgy leaders conferred. For once agreement came swiftly: they would force New Delhi, in the few remaining hours of its life, to relinquish the tape before it was buried under the wreckage of the regime.

The Indians were obdurate, at least until the fighters, scrambling off the carrier decks, made like a cloud of locusts for the subcontinent. The camel's back snapped; the tape was broadcast to the satellite network.

Televisions lit up policy rooms around the world; sweat dampened the shirts of the watchers. What if a teleport returned to Shanghai, or Los Angeles, or Rome? A tense, resentful public would lash out . . . possibly with the deep-gut fervor of Calcutta. Scrub as they might, the giant air machines couldn't filter out the stench of that fear.

Because if Calcutta was the rock, Wichita was the

hard place.

On the afternoon of 23 June 1979, five hours after the then-President of the US surrendered to end the Two Minute War, the Pukcip had staged a demonstration on the Kansas plain. Their small expeditionary force had slammed into Wichita with more fury than any tornado had ever unleashed; their grim sweep missed but four of the town's three hundred thousand residents. The rest lay rotting in the corngrowers' sun.

When it was over, their Commander had preempted the nation's communication networks. As cameras inched over the dark stains on the carapace he'd refused to cleanse, he said through his interpreter: "You see now our seriousness. Do as you are told, and all will be well. Oppose us even lightly, and a larger city will suffer the same fate."

Like a dynamite blast in a coal mine, Wichita crumbled America's solidity. While the last twitches of the President's feet were reflected in the gleaming tiles of a White House bathroom, politician after politician hurried to add his frightened constituency to the swelling list of those that would follow orders. By midnight the country had committed itself to cooperation.

Two years had passed since the headlines, the half-masted flags, the muffled drumbeats on Pennsylvania Avenue. The impact had yet to fade. The annual tribute of our or five widely separated children was clearly the lesser evil. They went so quickly, so completely . . . they left no bones to be washed by the summer rains . . . one could almost pretend that they, and the Pukcip, had never existed.

The alien presence on Earth was nearly invisible: a small embassy at the United Nations, regular equipment deliveries to the many Evaluation Centers, and an occasional spot-check of children reported to have been tested. Scientists were prohibited from examining them; even diplomats met them only at lengthy intervals.

They were strangers, and clever conquerors. Importing no overlords, advisors, or enforcers, they presented no targets. Like Mafiosi handing their victim a shovel, they made Terrans do the work. Any rebellion would have to attack the governments that traded a few children's futures for many citizens' lives.

Any successful rebel would have to raze the Centers, would have to cut off the steady trickle of teleports to Pukci.

Any such interruption would invite Pukcip retaliation on a scale that would dwarf Wichita and utterly discredit the rebels.

The options seemed stark to most leaders: they could protect escaping teleports, and be punished; or they could do nothing, be overthrown, and then watch their populaces be savaged.

In the gray light of dawn, with the sun only a band of pink promise on the horizon, the President reached his decision. America would continue to copperate with the Pukcip—up to a point. However, any returning children would find armed troops eager to defend them.

The men at the Cabinet meeting saw him hammer his fist on the long table, felt his agony of soul as though it were theirs, and shared his determination when he vowed: "No kid of ours goes to Pukci twice! Send in the Army."

§   §   §

Colonel Mark Hazard Olsen, spine straight as a pine from his native Vermont, meditated in the passenger seat of the Jeep. The wind, the smooth humming roar of the motor, the dawn-dappled rows of abandoned buildings, were all locked out of his thoughts. His entire being sought serenity.

Yet the housefly flitting of Pukcip warriors refused to respect the pattern and the peace of his mantra. He forced himself to persevere, but after a few minutes more opened his eyes. Maybe later, once the bright plating of his hunger had been corroded by hours of forced alertness, he could try again.

At the moment, all he wanted to do was kill a few Pukcip.

Olsen had been a major during the Two Minute War. When the Pukcip squad had wink-blinked onto his post, he'd been dictating a new page for the MP training manual. Scattered shots had drawn him to the window.

His uncomprehending blue eyes had seen the bright shells of the Pukcip, had seen the running, falling, sprawling blurs of khaki. More shots: a pitifully few steady growls punctuated by flurries of single cracks that seemed always to end in astonished screams of pain.

Hanging out the open window, he'd watched his men race for the armory, where all the weapons except the guards' were kept under lock and key. The first to emerge had taken cover, were waiting for the enemy to come carelessly into range. There! The machine gun roared, its tracers leaping out to the— but the foe was already gone, had already shielded itself inside a squad of stunned GI's.

"NO GRENADES!" he'd shouted. "NO GRE-NADES!" The din was too great for his order to be audible, but his men didn't need it. They wouldn't hurl indiscriminating death into their own ranks, not even to kill the commingling aliens.

The phone had rung; an enraged General had had to scream, "Surrender, you damn fool!" four times before its import had sunk in. A word to his secretary, a frantic realighment of intercom switches, and his hollow voice, pregnant with feedback squeal, had echoed through the firefights.

Afterwards the clean-up, as integral a part of modern warfare as hot turkey on Thanksgiving, or cold beer on the Fourth. Three hundred GI's lay dead and dying; another five hundred were wounded. In the pools of blood, under the half-wrecked armory, were found four bullet-riddled shells. The Pukcip, as contemptuous of their own dead as of the human living, had left them behind.

Olsen, after wondering what to do with them, had decided to ship them to a nearby university. He'd taken the alien weapons—the post had specialists who could say if they deserved detailed study—and then ordered a dozen sullen GI's to load the death-dulled shells onto a van.

Before the van had cleared the gate, the news of Wichita had crackled through every radio on the post. The GI's, without communication or negotiation, responded to the same instincts. They'd parked the van on the parade ground.

Gasoline burns hot and quick; Pukcip horn merely chars. The billows of black smoke had drawn the survivors, who'd contributed wood, and more gas, and phosphorus grenades. A wasp-bitter helicopter had offered a load of napalm. And through it all the men had stood, helpless rage under the dirty sweat of their empty-eyed faces. Among them was Mark Hazard Olsen, who'd waited till the last crisp curl of carapace had folded upon itself to give the order for bulldozed burial.

By then he'd been informed that his was one of the three US posts assaulted by the invaders. There had been no tactical or strategic reason for the attack— the motive had been psychological. Deliberately flaunting their ability to rain chaos on any defensive installation, the Pukcip had hoped to demoralize the military.

Their ploy had failed. Olsen had already started to work out tactics for the next engagement, tactics— the convoy jolted to a stop amid the potholes of a long-neglected parking lot; he dismounted and surveyed the old, two-story school building—which would be invaluable if the Pukcip came to Hartford.

§ § §

Ten minutes later, Walter F. Dortkowski, Director of the Hartford Evaluation Center, groaned aloud. The blacktop lawn of the commandeered school was littered with Jeeps, deuce-and-a-half's, and milling squads of soldiers. Cursing, he rammed his battered Volvo into his reserved space. Things weren't red-taped enough, they had to saddle him with the Army, too.

As he switched off the ignition, he brightened. Maybe the Governor, finally keeping her promise, had convinced the Army to take over. Maybe he could throw away his plasticized ID badge, break his clipboard over his knee, and go home a free man. God knew he'd tried to resign often enough before.

In July of 1979, when the Governor had named him Director, he'd accepted the appointment for two reasons, and on one condition. The condition had been that he'd step down within six months.

The reasons had been almost classically simple: first, a very important job had to be done with a minimum of time, money, and effort. Dortkowski, who had earned his MBA at Columbia before finding the fascination of educational administration, had realized—had been sweet-talked into realizing—that he could establish a better Center than any one else under consideration. The stakes had been too high for his hatred of the Pukcip to interfere. He'd felt—he'd been urged to feel—a responsibility to the public.

Then, once he'd truly understood—had been made to understand—how he could guarantee the safety of three and a half million people, the Governor had pulled out the plum: after six months of designing, implementing, and refining the evaluation system, he'd be named State Commissioner of Education. It would have been a wonderful 45th birthday present.

But difficulties arose. January, 1980: the administration could find no qualified successor, could he hold on for a few months more? Yes, he could. April, 1980: The Commissionership received too much exposure to be held by someone who symbolized Pukcip oppression; they'd find him another slot, but in the meantime . . . and the meantime became all the time, and the bars of inertia, animosity, and indispensability had grown around him like bamboo.

At last, I'm quitting! he'd declared, to the deputies and assistants and administrators who'd hemmed him in. He'd continued to say it; in the end, even to the Governor herself.

Warm sympathy had flowed across her face. Sadly, she'd told him she was sorry, she couldn't let him quit. She needed him too badly. And if he did just walk away from it, as he'd threatened to do, she personally had it in her power to make sure that he Never. Worked. Anywhere. At anything. Again. And in her face had glittered the eyes of a krait.

So he'd stayed, despite the vociferous hatred of people he'd never met, despite the pleas of his ostracized family. He'd stayed because he had no choice, because the Directorship—carrion-strewn plateau that it was—was his only pathway to the peak, and if he ever climbed down from it, they'd never let him near the mountain again.

Now, for the first time in months, a smile disturbed his sunken cheeks. Adjusting his tie, checking his frizzy gray hair in the rear-view mirror, he stepped into the early sun. Already the day felt hot. A shirtsleeve day. His small, neatly shod feet were light as he walked expectantly to the door. If he could transfer power quickly, he might have time for his fishing rod.

He might even get away before the first child arrived.

§ § §

Someone was shaking Jonathan's shoulder. It was his daddy, telling him to get up. He pushed his heavy eyelids open, but it was still dark. That meant it was going to rain a lot, 'less it was real early. Gradually, he remembered. Today he'd be 'valuated.

"You 'wake, boy?" gruffed his daddy.

"Yowp." It was true, too. He sat up, feeling alive and excited all over. "How soon we leaving, Daddy?"

"Soon's your mama fix us some breakfast. Get dressed, now."

"Okay, I be quick." He slid out from under the much-mended sheet, and started grabbing for the clothes his mama had laid out on his dresser. "I be real quick, Daddy. Don't wanna be late for my 'valuation.'" As he pulled on his underwear, he puzzled over his daddy's wordless turn and hasty exit.

§ . § §

Dortkowski stared into Olsen's face. Long and lean, dark from years of weather, lined by innumerable hard decisions, it was utterly impassive. Only two things hinted at the Colonel's feelings: the grinding of his teeth on the burnt-out stub of a cigar, and the ambiguous softness in his clear blue eyes.

"Sorry as hell to give you the wrong impression. Mr. Dortkowski," Olsen was saying. "We're here for one reason, and one reason only: to protect any kid who happens to come back from Pukci. We'll give you any assistance we can, but . . . we're not going to run your operation."

"It's my fault, Colonel." The words were very hard to get out. To be trapped in reality's field after free-falling through fantasy like a wide-eyed child . . . a glider pilot must feel the same, when he's lost the thermals and the ground is rushing up at him. "Thanks for, uh, letting me down easy."

He turned away. Hands behind his back, shoulders slumped, he entered the I-shaped school building. The place would consume him yet. Already it had cost him his friends, his reputation as a concerned administrator . . . what next? His wife? His life? Olsen had said his Calcutta counterpart had been torn to pieces by an enraged mob. That might be better. One white-hot moment of pure, unmasked hatred—despite the agonies of dying—might be preferable to years of uncomfortable silences, of embarrassed breakings-off.

Hand kneading his belly, where the ulcer had awakened with its usual rumbling torment, he trudged down the stem of the I. As he did every morning, he paused by the door that led to the

memory-wiping machinery. That had earned him more abuse than anything else.

The test could be invalidated if the children knew what to expect, so the Pukcip had designed equipment to keep the already-screened from describing it to the untested. There had yet to be a single adverse reaction to the erasing—if nothing else, the Pukcip were unparalleled in neuroelectronics—but every mother despised him for exposing her child's mind to a callous alien machine.

The dials glittered in the slanting sunlight. If only the scales were larger; if only the gauges measured months instead of minutes . . . to go in, to strip his brain of its experience, to tear from it the skills that made him indispensable to the political establishment . . . they'd have to let him resign, then. They'd have no use for a seventeen-year-old mind in a forty-six-year-old body . . .

He unlocked the door to his office. The small cubicle smelled of arguments and dust, of hysteria and decay. He forced a swollen window up six inches, as high as it would go. Rubbing the neck muscle that had protested the exertion, he dropped into the chair behind his desk.

On the blotter lay a computer printout naming the 250 children who would pass through the building that day. The coldly efficient type face hit him like a slap in the face. Lowering his head to his crossed arms, he wished he could be as pragmatic about it as the Colonel was.

§ § §

Olsen was stationing his men just outside the projection room. His blue eyes, as if belying Dortkowski's assessment, held real anger whenever they glanced through the next doorway.

"They were too slow in Calcutta," he was telling his lieutenant. "They gawked like raw recruits while the Puks took the kid back. I won't put up with that kind of horseshit. The odds are against its happening here—that was Calcutta's third or fourth teleport, and this Center hasn't even had one yet—but if it does, so help me God, you'll either save the child or face a firing squad." He removed his cigar and spat out a shred of tobacco for emphasis. "Do I make myself clear?"

"Perfectly, sir." The lieutenant was relaxed but watchful: he knew Olsen prized performance above all else. "Are there any limitations on what weapons we may use, sir?"

Olsen studied the dingy anteroom before replying. A touch of claustrophobia flicked him from a distance, warned him of the oppressiveness it could bring to bear.

The ceiling sagged in the middle; any significant explosion would bring it down on everyone's head. "No grenades." Even a firefight would weaken it, perhaps disastrously. "Sidearms and M-16's only." He'd have to risk it, no matter what memories it teased into life.

In 'Nam once, during his first tour on the Delta, he'd led a company of men into a subterranean vc arms cache. An observer silent in a treetop had pressed the button of a small radio transmitter; the plastique had gone up and the tunnel roof had come down. The memory of muffled screams, of tattered fingernails clawing at soggy earth, still haunted Olsen.

But now it had competition: the tape he'd seen over closed-circuit TV that morning would stalk his dreams for months to come.

"There's one advantage to his kind of confined space," he said to his lieutenant. "They won't be able to ride their carousel."

Films of the Two Minute War had revealed distinct patterns—predictable patterns—in the Pukcip style of skirmishing. Each warrior moved through a standard series of positions, a series as immutable as an 18th Century waltz. To defeat them on the battlefield, a foe had merely to determine each warrior's starting point, and fire there a fraction of a second before the Pukcip was due to materialize.

That called for a special soldier: one who could make sense of the shifting, surging intermingling of gaudy shells and faded khaki; one who could synchronize his trigger squeezes with the rhythm of their maneuvers; one who could stand fast even when a Pukcip blinked into the space next to him.

Olsen had asked for permission to select and train an elite detachment of such soldiers. Civilian eyebrows had lifted—there was no future, they thought, in preparing to fight an enemy that could depopulate a continent if it chose—but the political pressure to develop contingency plans had meshed with the Pentagon's desire for revenge. He had received his colonelcy.

"Two last things," Olsen said, staring at the cracked plaster of the anteroom walls. "First, make sure you rotate your men, keep 'em fresh. Those idiots in Calcutta were probably asleep on their feet."

"Consider it done, sir."

"Second, if a kid shows up, aim above his head and hose the room. That should catch the Puks by surprise, and leave 'em no place to jump except back home. All right?"

"Yes, sir."

"Carry on." The far doorway called him. Scowling, he crossed to it, and scanned the holographic projection of the—reception room? laboratory? zoo?—on Pukci. All shimmers of swirling blues and purples, it stood in haughty contrast to the peeling green paint of the Center. Olsen glared at the metallic glints in the odd-shaped tiles of its floor, as if he could dissolve the deception through sheer force of will. The vivid image remained unaltered. The Pukcip equipment was too good.

Spurred by an impulse as inexplicable as fate, he stepped forward. The lieutenant's surprised gasp plucked at his shoulder, but he didn't respond. He had no time. Gravity grasped him, ripped him through the planes of colored light. An instant later, he was bouncing softly on the nylon mesh strung beneath the doorway.

Damn effective, he thought. *If I hadn't known—if I'd been a trusting six year-old—I'd have expected it to be solid. Shit, even knowing, I was startled.*

A child's world is tinged with the mysterious and the irrational. To him, fantasy is merely fact in which he can not participate. What looks like a room must be a room, if he can enter it.

Two hundred fifty children ran, skipped, hopped, or walked into the Puckip projection every day. Passage over the threshhold triggered the test which, for one uncaring nanosecond, pitted the law of gravity against the child's belief that he was in a room whose floor could support his weight. If reality won, the testee tumbled; if faith overrode it to write its own version of natural law, the child either levitated in blissful ignorance . . . or teleported directly to the original room, somewhere on Pukci.

Roughly eleven of every million testees had faith enough to warp reality.

§ § §

Jonathan was in the front seat, between his mama and his daddy. He'd wanted to ride in the back—both his parents were pretty big, and there wasn't much room. They'd told him that just that once they wanted to be together. It was sort of nice to be able

59

to lean against his mama's softness, but there wasn't any air. If he were sitting where he always sat, the wind would be buffeting his face, and he'd have to half-close his eyes, which made the whole world look different.

"Is it long time, Daddy?" he asked.

"Most an hour, boy." He took his eyes off the road and gazed down at his only son. "Don't be in such a hurry, y'hear? We gonna get there, we just gonna have to sit and wait till they ready for us anyhow."

Jonathan nodded solemnly. He'd been wanting to ask his daddy why he was driving so much slower than usual.

§　§　§

The stone floor was worn; Olsen's combat boots set up a hollow ringing. The old school building had, at that hour of the morning, the semi-deserted air of a shut-down refinery. It was hard to believe how crowded the empty corridors would become; harder still to think how many people had passed through them in either of the building's two lifetimes, ironic that each involved some sort of screening.

The silence was almost good. Dortkowski's crew would shatter it within the next half hour, but the first children weren't due till nine o'clock, more than an hour away. That would be time enough to look things over, to smooth out the jangle of this thoughts. It bothered him that he would have to stand idle while the Pukcip equipment assayed the value of two hundred fifty children.

He left-faced into the main wing. Rickety metal folding chairs lined the walls; he repositioned one that had wandered out a few feet. A stencil on the seat's underside declared it to be the property of a local funeral home. Disgusted, he kicked it. The impact chipped paint off the crumbly cinderblocks; quarter-sized flakes of green skittered down to the baseboard.

Damn the Pukcip for their ability to teleport. And damn the civilians for being so easily cowed! The

Army could have taken them, once it had recovered from the initial shock. Their weapons weren't very good, no matter what the hysterical media claimed, and the carouselling warriors took longer to aim than a GI did. If their tiny expeditionary force hadn't held most of the government hostage . . .

The fact that every other officer in the world had succumbed to the same ruse didn't lessen the shame. If anything, it heightened it. A professional respects his opposite numbers, often to the point of judging himself by his perception of how well he could do against them. When not a single human officer proves himself capable of beating off a handful of stalk-eyed child thieves . . .

Only revenge could remove the stigma. But the Pukcip were immune—Earth neither knew where Pukci was, nor had the star drive to get troops there. In a year or two, though . . .

The US and the USSR were co-developing a faster-than-light drive. If it were possible, if it weren't a mirage hanging stubbornly above the horizon, they'd launch a grim fleet and ransack space for Pukci. Fueled by a bitterness that wouldn't fade with the generations, they'd find it, and avenge Wichita, Lyons, Serpukhov, all the other demonstration cities . . . the Pukcip warriors could dance quadrilles on the asteroids, but their planet wouldn't be able to dodge the swollen tips of the nuclear missiles.

One fear dogged Olsen, as it did everyone who hungered for satisfaction: if an FTL drive could be invented, why were the Pukcip allowing work on it to continue?

If it couldn't be invented, why had the joint communique announcing the project provoked the invasion?

It was obvious, in the crystallized brilliance of hindsight, that the Pukcip had spied on Earth for years. They'd done nothing to reveal themselves until the release of the joint communique, but within twelve hours of that first, hope-stirring news flash, the four-armed teleports had stormed the world.

Olsen had his own theory: that the Pukcip theoreticians had decided FTL *travel* was impossible, but that research into it would somehow uncover natural teleports. So the Pukcip warriors, as edgily suspicious as military men anywhere, had opted to remove Earth's teleports before they could spearhead an invasion of Pukci.

That fit neatly with the intelligence analysis that only the enemy's soldiers could teleport. If, in their culture, the power had purely military applications, their experts would naturally have decided that Earth would also exploit it for war.

They were afraid, Olsen thought. *They knew that once we started roaming the stars, we'd find them ... shit, and I thought we were xenophobic. Or maybe they know how xenophobic we are, and figured they'd eliminate our space capability before we'd discovered we had it ... or maybe their motive is completely different—like they wanted to maximize the return on their investment, and so they held off while our population grew, until it seemed that we were ready to find, and use, the raw materials they needed* ... he gave up the effort at triple-think with a tired shake of his head. The *why* of the situation didn't really matter, not to him. The specialists could worry about it.

His job was to be ready to fight them.

His hope was that he'd get the chance.

§ § §

Dortkowski lifted his clipboard, recorded the Center's need for more Pukcip ink, and looked the room over one more time. Everything seemed to be ready for the children. The question was, would he be ready for the parents?

He'd explained it ten thousand times himself; he'd had every newspaper in the state run articles on it; he'd even scraped together the funds for a brochure distributed at the door. But still they screamed their outrage when they saw the tricolored tattoo on their children's wrists.

What could he say that he hadn't said before? Clearly the best thing was simply to start up the mental tape recorder, let the tired neutral words fall as they had so often before, and then wear the stoic face while spittle spattered his cheeks.

The Pukcip wanted their slag heaps labeled. What else could he say? To tell a mother that her child likes something she doesn't is to incite the hurricane; to tell a father that the process is painless is to ignore the very real hurt he feels at his child's disfigurement.

The bureaucrat had but one defense: *I'm sorry, it's not my idea, I didn't make that rule, if it were up to me I wouldn't, I can't make an exception, I'm sorry, but I'm just following orders.* His ulcer pinched, as if to extend the range of his soul pain. It was a lousy defense and he knew it. The fact that every word was true made him no happier.

What the parents couldn't understand was what he didn't dare forget: any deviation from the Pukcip procedures might be discovered in one of the irregular Pukcip spotchecks. Such a discovery could condemn an entire city.

The headache was starting up again; his ink-stained fingers massaged the bulging vein in his temple. It was going to be one of those days . . . but maybe he'd get lucky. Maybe a parent would get infuriated enough to put him into the hospital.

Immediately he sighed. That was wishful thinking. There was always an aide, a cop, *somebody* to step in officiously and protect him from the lesser suffering. Why would no one do it for the greater?

His hands groped for the center drawer of his desk: warped wood screeched as he pulled it out. It overflowed with the debris of bureaucracy: forms, stamp pads, pencils . . . brushing them to one side, he uncovered the small green bottle. He shook it. The lethal white pills rattled like castanets.

They were his ticket out. If the Center uncovered a

teleport—no, *when* it did, because eventually it had to—he'd screw off the top, tilt back the bottle, and empty dusty release down his throat . . . because it would have been his fault. Without his administrative expertise, it never would have happened . . . and he could see no other means of atonement.

Then he laughed, sourly, and the acid bit at the back of his throat. Atonement? He knew himself better. It was escape, the modern man's escape: swallow the pills and dodge the pain. Let chemistry exorcise reality. Let death deny his responsibility for losing a child to the Pukcip pipeline.

§ § §

They were driving straight at the sun, and if it didn't rise up off the end of the road before they got there, they were going to have a whole lot of trouble getting to his 'valuation.

Jonathan squirmed around so the bright streaks wouldn't be flying into his eyes. Catching his mama looking down at him, he asked the question that had been floating around in his head for the last couple days. "Mama, why they wanna 'valuate me for anyway?"

"They doing it to all the little children, honey."

"But how come they want *me,* Mama?"

"Cause the government say you gotta."

"Oh." He considered that for a moment, then shrugged. If his daddy listened to the government, whoever that was, he guessed he'd better, too. Sure didn't sound like his mama like that guy, though. Her voice had done the same thing to "government" that it always did to "landlord."

§ § §

Olsen strode through a classroom to a window above the parking lot. The April day was going to be hot; a tang of soft asphalt was beginning to permeate the air. Below, the unseasonably cruel sun tormented a cluster of anxious parents. They probably hadn't slept all night. Unable to stand the suspense, they'd come early, to get it over with quickly. Poor bastards.

Their faces were as gray as Dortkowski's hair.

The odds were against any of them losing a kid—from the initial statistics, only one in a million could teleport—in fact, they were ten times more likely to go home with a levitator. Still, the possibility that their child might wind up a nugget in a Pukcip pocket was enough to make most of them despair.

Leaning on the dusty windowsill, he clenched his teeth. He had a boy of his own—Ralph, four years old, now. In less than two years' time he'd be shuffling through the corridors of a Center much like this, one more big-eyed kid in a line that stretched all the way back to the world's maternity wards. As a father, he knew that the most nerve-wracking aspect was that if your kid should go to Pukci, you'd never know what they did to him.

Not that Calcutta wasn't giving him some very nasty ideas.

He couldn't decide whether he should tell Grace about the video-tape. If one of the networks was leaked a copy, of course, he wouldn't have to, but if its icy horror kept it off the air . . . *could* he tell her?

No. From a comment or two dropped into her conversations, he knew she was expecting him to find and pull the string that would exempt Ralph. He'd explained, more than once, that there was no such string—that even the President's grandson had endured the evaluation—but she behaved as though she'd never heard him.

It was either acute tunnel vision—she saw what she wanted to see, and no more—or she had a very touching faith in him.

Straightening, brushing the dust off his hands, Olsen gazed into the sky. He wouldn't tell her. There was always the random factor to consider—why make her fret for two years if there was even the slightest chance that the armies of Earth could hurl themselves against the Pukcip warriors?

If it didn't happen, she'd wax hysterical while Ralph was being tested, but once he came through alive she'd calm down.

If it did happen ... either the Centers would be leveled by jubilant wrecking crews, or there'd be no citizens to fill their halls.

§ § §

"We here," his daddy grunted. "Looks like they just opening the doors."

"Jonathan, child—" suddenly his mama turned sideways, and her soft round eyes practically swallowed up his own "—you gonna be all right, honey, y'hear?"

"Yowp." His head bobbed up and down, till he twisted to see his daddy, who cleared his throat with embarrassing loudness. "You all right, Daddy?"

"Just fine, boy." He pushed his door open, but before he threw his long legs into the parking lot, he gave Jonathan his hand. "Do what they tell you, boy, and everything's gonna be okay."

Jonathan didn't say anything. He was too busy wondering what they were so nervous about.

§ § §

Olsen stood by the door to the anteroom, eyes restless, muscles panther-loose. Facing him was Dortkowski, thin frame draped in a soft white lab coat. Behind him was the Specialist 5th Class who ran the communications gear. It was a mild reassurance to know that if anything happened, the entire chain of command would hear of it within seconds. It was less reassuring to recall that the Calcutta guards had had exactly seven seconds in which to react.

He glanced at Dortkowski, whose bony hand was massaging his stomach. Evidently the tension was gnawing at the Director. It was understandable: the children came so slowly; the parents hovered so watchfully. From the other's impatient checking of his watch, Olsen guessed that they'd fallen behind schedule. Any further delays would probably drive Dortkowski into a nervous fit.

The short, shabby corridor seemed to quiver with an air of expectancy. Everyone was uptight, jerking about at the slightest noise, as if convinced that It was going to happen. Eventually, of course, it would. The only question was when.

Dortkowski's statistics were no help. They said one in a million, but refused to say which of those million it would be. He'd have to imitate the bureaucrat: test them all, hold his breath on each, and—if he was there long enough—swig the Maalox after every five or six. Olsen knew, with a pawn's despair, that even when they lost one, he wouldn't be able to relax. Though there would be only two in two million, they could come consecutively.

He wondered what was in Dortkowski's other pocket, the one he patted every few minutes. It wasn't ulcer medicine. The outlined bottle was too small.

Fighting back the temptation to pace, he leaned against the wall. He had to be near enough to hear the voice patterns echo through the anteroom.

First the flare of fright as the child fell, then a gasp, then bewilderment rushing to the brink of tears. If the costumed clown by the safety net caught the kid's attention quickly, the thin, confused voice would switch to giggles in mid-sob. If not, they had to hold everything until the child was safely inside, out of earshot of the next testee.

A little black boy was walking towards him. All dressed up, with his shoes shined and his hair in a neat Afro, he looked scared. He was probably getting too much attention. All the adults were eyeing him, and their expressions would be hard for a kid to read. But his jaw was set, and he put one foot in front of the other with praiseworthy determination.

Dortkowski smiled down at the boy, which seemed to help a little, and one of the black soldiers winked. His voice was still tiny, though, when he said his name was Jonathan. Yes, sir; he'd go into the next room and wait.

Olsen watched his small back pass through the rainbow doorway. As he braced himself for the cry of

betrayal, his back tingled. The boy was too quiet. The air smelled ... odd, and its pressure seemed to have dropped.

Barely noticing the green bottle in Dortkowski's hand, he looked. Jonathan was standing on glistening tiles, apparently inspecting the spacious room. Doors opened in the shiny walls; Olsen saw Pukcip heads come around the edges. The boy sat down and started to sob.

Dortkowski gave a sound, almost a whimper, of relief, and sagged against him, murmuring, "It's a levita—"

But Olsen shouted, "Hell with that, it's a space warp! Get in there, you bastards, *get in there and take that place!!!*"

Within seconds, his and other booted feet were skidding across Pukcip stone; back in Hartford, his Spec 5 was demanding reinforcements for the bridgehead; and Olsen, automatic in hand, was cradling the terrified boy.

§ § §

Jonathan was frantic to know what he'd done wrong. After all, they'd *told* him to go into the room, even though they must have known how far away it was. It was very confusing. If they knew he couldn't go there, why did they get so excited when he brought there here?

§ § §

With almost clinical dispassion, Dortkowski watched his skinny fingers tighten the cap on the bottle. He'd come *that* close. He almost hadn't had the courage to look. If Olsen's uncompromising eyes hadn't swept over him . . .

They should have guessed. When the test provoked two different paranormal reactions, one less common than the other, they should have guessed that it might provoke a third, even more rare. This boy, neither levitator nor teleport, was something else entirely: a talent capable of wedding Earth to Pukcip via another dimension, and of keeping them joined, perhaps indefinitely. Continued testing might eventually have uncovered a fourth kind of power . . . but he didn't have time for that, not now.

Though the halls were a blur, he knew he should clear them for the Army. He walked up to the crowd of parents and children, spread his arms, said, "That's all, folks, it's all over, go on home, there won't be any more evaluations."

And the tears on his cheeks made his smile more profound.

§ § §

The war was short, and perhaps more savage than it should have been, but no one knew how long Jonathan could hold open the doorway. Besides, the once humbled generals wanted an unconditional surrender, and quick. And more than a few of the infantrymen had had friends or relatives in Wichita.

The Pukcip contributed heavily to their own defeat. Most of their tiny army was elsewhere, and had to be recalled. By the time it was ready to skirmish, a thousand GI's had spread throughout the neighborhood. The entire 82nd Airborne was in position before the aliens had deduced the existence, and the location, of the doorway. Their assault on it ran headlong into Olsen's special forces, and was repulsed with heavy casualties.

Furious, humiliated, and totally unaccustomed to defensive warfare, the Pukcip wasted the little strength they had. They launched a dozen vindictive raids on Terran cities, and lost soldiers in each. Then, before their terrorism could take effect, their panic-stricken government called them home. Ordered to destroy the invaders, they tried—but pent-up hatred and sheer numbers more than cancelled their carouselling multiplicity. With the arrival of the 101st Airborne, the battles tapered into sniper attacks, and those into silence.

If they'd reacted less emotionally—if they'd had any experiences with invasions—if they'd studied Russian or Chinese military history . . . but they hadn't, so the war was short. And perhaps more savage than it should have been.

The Army took two sets of documents from Pukcip archives before closing the doorway on chaos.

The first included blueprints for a functioning starship.

The second included invoices for FTL drive units sold to the shipyards on Rigel VI. Each unit was identified by its city of origin. Four had come from Calcutta.

BACKSPACE
by F. M. Busby

> *Mr. Busby is graying, bearded, and*
> *cheerfully bouncy. Like Jack Haldeman*
> *and your editor, he once had a major*
> *part in putting on a World Science*
> *Fiction Convention (Seattle in 1961:*
> *the SeaCon), but seems to be recovering*
> *nicely by now. An electrical engineer*
> *by training, he spent many years with*
> *the Alaska Communications System before*
> *turning to full-time writing.*

The beard and overflowing hair would have fooled me—but who else comes visiting, late on a Monday afternoon, with a six-pack of canned Martinis? So I opened the door.

He lifted a finger to the probable location of his lips. "An important datum, friend Peter—I do not exist."

I shook hands and thought about it. Sam's only flaky until you figure out what he means; then the term becomes understatement.

I closed the door behind him and said, "Then who does?" Realizing I'd asked a poor question, I rephrased it. "I mean, who just came in here, wearing your skin?"

He nodded. "A debatable point. Let us repair to your kitchen and debate it." He led the way, opened the refrigerator and exchanged his six-pack for two beers, one of which he handed to me. "For now, Petrus Sapiens, think of me as an astral body—a refugee from the material world."

He sat, and I across the table. "For a while there," I said, "I was beginning to think you *didn't* exist. After you cleared up our smog problem here—and I haven't had a chance to thank you—"

He waved a hand. "De nada—a simple matter of editing."

I couldn't agree. Reversing the Earth's rotation, to switch the prevailing winds and blow the city's pollution the other way? Not that I'd realized, immediately, what had happened—but then I noticed that the books say the Sun rises in the East, when obviously the opposite is true . . .

"How did you do it, anyway?"

He shrugged. "How should I know? I don't have the scientific mind." He fetched a Martini to set beside his beer. As in the old days, he sprinkled a powder into it and stirred until the stuff dissolved. I've never asked him what it is.

From under the low-hanging hair his eyebrows appeared and made a frown. "Something about a macrospin being the resultant of microspins—I read that someplace, and it sounds good. So I just spun the electrons in my head the other way, all at once, and the effect spread. You ever do anything like that, Pete?"

"Not on purpose," I said. "But why did you disappear?"

The brows rose to hide again. "Think about it. How did you find out what I did?" He nodded. "Lousy editing, is what. I forgot to fix the records, to match. So before the government could put a lid on me, I ran for cover."

"But how would they know—?"

He sipped the Martini and grimaced. "You can't get real zouch any more, but this stuff I put in here isn't half bad." I waited; he said, "Well, I edit freelance, you know—and sometimes for the gum'mint, even. You remember the Kairenger scandal?" I shook my head.

"Of course you don't," said Sam. "I edited it out, that's why. And lived three years on the proceeds—my fee." He sighed. "But they knew, Peter the Great—they had the handle on me. And to be utterly frank, this minor chore here, for your convenience—

it was somewhat in breach of contract."

His next sip of Martini must have been heavy with zouch, whatever that is, for his eyes bulged. He gulped some beer. Still breathing hard, he said, "I am not given, Pieter, to maundering diatribes about ethics; I see myself as a practical man in an impractical world. So the question was rather simple."

"It was?" Thinking: *what* question?

"Of a surety. Whether to edit the government, with its threat to me, out of my life—or me out of its. I chose the latter."

"And so—"

"That's why I no longer exist. *Much* simpler."

I needed another beer. So would he, soon—I brought him one, and said, "Well, then—who *is* here, and why? I mean, I'm always glad to see you, and all that, but—"

He lit a cigar; I provided an ashtray. He said, "Through these eyes, Pedro, many of me look out—and ever have. Didn't you know?"

Well, Sam's mind always did have more independent parts than a jigsaw puzzle. I nodded. "Right now, which one's taking a peek?"

He finished the Martini, opened another, dusted and stirred it. One sip—his mustache rippled; I think he smiled. "Much better, Petrov. Either I have the combination or my taste buds have agreed to fake it." He waved a hand; cigar ash scattered.

"Question of identity," he said. "Who am I, and you also? Oh, I know—you remain yourself, changing only within moderate limits. Monotonous, I'd find it—but whatever flips your switches."

His eyes narrowed, closed, then opened wide. I waited, and he said, "I'm taking a vote. How else?" Then he laughed. "It's a tie between a name I dislike and one I can't pronounce. The hell with it—call me Sam, and hope this place isn't bugged."

§ § §

He'd changed, Sam had—and not only in appearance. The lazy voice was now brisk, yet still the mind

73

dealt in caution. Not until his third Martini would he speak of purpose. Then suddenly he ground his cigar into the tray until both ceased to smolder, and said, "I've found, Pietro, a new way to edit—day by day, cautiously observing, proceeding by trial and thus reducing error."

"As you used to say—chickenly?"

"Indeed—and now, more so than ever. With a modern touch of gadgetry, to aid—" From a pocket he brought out a small, oblong device—black, studded with lights and buttons. After a moment I recognized it as an electronic perpetual calendar—with additions that somehow didn't surprise me.

"What does that thing do?"

He handed it to me. "Look for yourself—but don't touch the grey button. Today, I've already put in good order." I looked but said nothing; I felt my eyebrows heading north.

"Obviously," he said, "my contrivance indicates the date. Or else," and he opened a fresh beer for himself, "it *sets* the date. An interesting philosophical question, really. Every action has an equal and opposite reaction. Do you know who said that?"

"Sir Isaac Newton?"

"In a limited sense, I suppose." He lit another cigar. "I was thinking of Manfred the Witless, an obscure Varangian chieftain of a century best left alone. The one valid memento of his entire reign."

I shook my head. "How did he get into this? And what's the business you said, about this thing *setting* the date?"

Using the unlit end of his cigar he stirred the Martini, then licked powder specks from the damp stub. "Manfred came to power through his mother's side of the family—necessarily so, since no one would admit to being his father. And then—" He paused. "Oh, yes—I see what you mean. Well, it's the grey button. No—*don't* touch it."

"The grey button?"

"Yes. It's—well, you might call it a backspace key."

§ § §

I've never caught Sam in an exaggeration. The occasional lie, yes—exaggerations, never. Still, I had to test his claim—and said so.

"Very well, Peter the Skeptical. Let us see—" He looked at his watch. "I arrived here, I believe, at twelve minutes past five. Tomorrow at that time— you will be home?" I nodded. "Then I leave the device here with you. And at that exact point of tomorrow, twelve past five, you push the grey button."

§ § §

Traffic was heavy that Tuesday, but shortly after five I reached home. At the proper moment, I followed Sam's instruction. Then I heard a knock at the door and went to answer it.

The beard and overflowing hair would have fooled me—but who else comes visiting, late on a Monday afternoon, with a six-pack of canned Martinis?

Monday? But it had been . . .

I opened the door anyway.

§ § §

He was into his second Martini before we talked. I wasn't sulking—I simply couldn't think what to say. Finally, "Sam? It could be—it *should* be—that you're just here two days in a row. So how come—how is it that I *know* we've got Monday on reruns?"

For a time he didn't answer. I guessed the line was busy, to his other head you can't see. Then he said, "There's a *Mondayness* to Monday—you sense it, do you, Peter-san? Not to be mistaken. For centuries I could lie in my unforeseeable tomb, and when Gabriel—most likely portrayed by Louis Armstrong—blew his riff, I would rise in all my dank skeletal dignity. And I would wonder—why the hell did he have to rouse me on a *Monday?*" He nodded; his Martini wet his beard.

There are things it doesn't pay to ask Sam—but I was curious. "In that case, O Nonexistent One, why did you feel the need to *repeat* Monday?"

His eyebrows did their vanishing act; behind the mustache curtain I thought I saw a gleam of smile. "It is, Piterluk of the Analytical Bent, that I am broke. So I have a job, an employment that pays me—no, not in peanuts, even, but rather in the shells of peanuts."

He drained his Martini. "And Monday happens to be my day off."

§ § §

Time passed. My wife Carla returned from visiting her grandmother in Sacramento. We had a great reunion. Sam pushed the button—the grey one. My wife Carla returned from visiting her grandmother in Sacramento. We had a greater reunion.

The president spoke on three TV networks and announced a new sure-fire plan to halt inflation. The next day, a Tuesday, prices rose an average of twenty percent. Sam pushed the grey button. The president spoke on three networks and announced a new sure-fire plan to keep his hands out of the economy. The next day, a Tuesday, prices rose an average of five percent. Sam pushed the grey button . . .

§ § §

All in all, Sam's button works rather well. Any time he starts getting too many changes for the worse, he plays it safe and leaves bad enough alone. He says the reason I notice, while others don't, is that since I've used the gadget once, now I'm tuned to it.

Maybe he's right. But I do wish he'd get himself a new job—or at least a different day off.

I'm getting pretty damned tired of Monday.

PERCHANCE TO DREAM
by Sally A. Sellers

*This story, Sally Sellers's first sale, is the result
of a writing workshop at the University of
Michigan, headed by Lloyd Biggle, Jr. The
author tells us that she wrote for as long as she
can remember, but wrote only for creative
writing courses while in college. Since
graduation, she worked as a waitress, traveled
in Europe, and worked as a medical
technician in hematology. She now lives with
her family, two cats, and about a hundred
plants, and is a research assistant
at the University of Michigan.*

From the playground came the sound of laughter.

A gusty night wind was sweeping the park, and
the light at the edge of the picnic grounds swung
crazily. Distorted shadows came and went, rushing
past as the wind pushed the light to the end of its
arc, then sliding back jerkily.

Again the laughter rang out, and this time Norb
identified the creaking sound that accompanied it.
Someone was using the swing. Nervously he peered
around the swaying branches of the bush, but he saw
no one.

He heard a click. Danny had drawn his knife. Hastily Norb fumbled for his own. The slender weapon
felt awkward in his hand, even after all the hours of
practice.

"It'll be easy," Danny had said. "There's always
some jerk in the park after dark—they never learn."
Norb shivered and gripped the knife more tightly.

Then he saw them—a young couple walking hand
in hand among the trees. Danny chuckled softly, and
Norb relaxed somewhat. Danny was right—this
would be a cinch.

"You take the girl," Danny whispered.

Norb nodded. All they had to do was wait—the couple was headed right toward them. They were high school kids, no more than fifteen or sixteen, walking slowly with their heads together, whispering and giggling. Norb swallowed and tensed himself.

"Now!" Danny hissed.

They were upon them before the kids had time to react. Danny jerked the boy backward and threw him to the ground. Norb grabbed the back of the girl's collar and held his knife at her throat.

"Okay, just do what we say and nobody gets hurt," snarled Danny. He pointed his knife at the boy's face. "You got a wallet, kid?"

The boy stared in mute terror at the knife. The girl made small whimpering sounds in her throat, and Norb tightened his hold on her collar.

"Come on, come on! Your wallet!"

From somewhere in the shadows, a woman's voice rang out. "Leave them alone!"

Norb whirled as a dark form charged into Danny and sent him sprawling. Oh God, he thought, we've been caught! As the boy leaped to his feet and started to run, Norb made a futile swipe at him with his knife. His grip on the girl must have relaxed, because she jerked free and followed the boy into the woods.

Norb looked from the retreating kids to the two wrestling figures, his hands clenched in indecision. The dark form had Danny pinned to the ground. He was squirming desperately, but he couldn't free himself. "Get her off me!" he cried.

"Jesus!" Norb whispered helplessly. The kids had begun to scream for help. They'd rouse the whole neighborhood.

"Norb!" screamed Danny.

It was a command, and Norb hurled himself onto the woman. Twice he stabbed wildly at her back, but she only grunted and held on more tightly. He struck out again, and this time his knife sank deeply into soft flesh. Spurting blood soaked his hand and sleeve, and he snatched them away in horror.

Danny rolled free. He got to his feet, and the two of them stood looking down at the woman. The knife was buried in the side of her throat.

"Oh my God," whimpered Norb.

"You ass!" cried Danny. "Why didn't you just pull her off? You killed her!"

Norb stood paralyzed, staring down at the knife and the pulsing wound. Fear thickened in his throat, and he felt his stomach constrict. He was going to be sick.

"You better run like hell. You're in for it now."

Danny was gone. Norb wrenched his gaze from the body. On the other side of the playground, the kids were still calling for help. He saw car lights up by the gate, swinging into the park drive.

Norb began to run.

The gush of blood from the wound slowed abruptly and then stopped. The chest heaved several times with great intakes of air. Then it collapsed, and a spasm shook the body. In the smooth motion of a slowly tightening circle, it curled in on itself. The heart gave three great beats, hesitated, pumped once more, and was still.

Norb caught up with Danny at the edge of the woods. They stopped, panting, and looked in the direction of the car. It had come to a stop by the tennis courts, and, as they watched, the driver cut his motor and turned off his lights.

"This way," whispered Danny. "Come on."

As they headed across the road for the gate, the car's motor suddenly started. Its lights came on, and it roared into a U-turn to race after them.

"It's the cops!" Danny yelled. "Split up!"

Norb was too frightened. Desperately he followed Danny, and the pair of them fled through the gate and turned along the street as the patrol car swung around the curve. Then Danny veered off, and Norb followed him through bushes and into a back yard. A dog began yelping somewhere. Danny scaled a fence and dropped into the adjoining back yard, and Norb followed, landing roughly and falling to his knees.

He scrambled to his feet and collided with Danny, who was laughing softly as he watched the patrol car. It had turned around and was headed back into the park.

The heart had not stopped. It was pumping—but only once every six minutes, with a great throb. At each pulse, a pinprick of light danced across the back of the eyelids. The wound attempted to close itself and tightened futilely around the intrusion of steel. A neck muscle twitched. Then another, but the knife remained. The tissue around the blade began contracting minutely, forcing it outward in imperceptible jerks.

Officer Lucas parked near the playground and started into the trees. He could not have said what he was looking for, but neighbors had reported hearing cries for help, and the way those two punks had run told him they'd been up to something. He switched on his flashlight, delineating an overturned litter basket that had spewed paper across the path. The gusting wind tore at it, prying loose one fluttering fragment at a time. Cautiously he walked forward. Gray-brown tree trunks moved in and out of the illumination as he crept on, but he could see nothing else.

He stumbled over an empty beer bottle, kicked it aside, and then stopped uncertainly, pivoting with his light. It revealed nothing but empty picnic tables and cold barbecue grills, and he was about to turn back when his beam picked out the body, curled motionless near a clump of bushes. Lucas ran forward and knelt beside the woman, shining his light on her face.

The throat wound seemed to have stopped bleeding, but if the knife had sliced the jugular vein—he leaned closer to examine the laceration. Belatedly a thought occurred to him, and he reached for the wrist. There was no pulse. He shone his light on the chest, but it was motionless.

Lucas got to his feet and inspected the area hastily. Seeing no obvious clues, he hurried back to the patrol car.

The heart throbbed again, and another pinprick of light jumped behind the woman's eyelids. The tissues in the neck tightened further as new cells developed, amassed, and forced the blade a fraction of an inch outward. The wounds in the back, shallow and clean, had already closed. The lungs expanded once with a great intake of air. The knife jerked again, tilted precariously, and finally fell to the ground under its own weight. Immediately new tissue raced to fill the open area.

The radio was squawking. Lucas waited for the exchange to end before picking up the mike. "Baker 23."

"Go ahead, Baker 23."

"I'm at Newberry Park, east end. I've got a 409 and request M.E."

"Confirmed, 23."

"Notify the detective on call."

"Clear, 23."

"Ten-four." He hung up the mike and glanced back into the woods. Probably an attempted rape, he thought. She shouldn't have fought. The lousy punks! Lucas rubbed his forehead fretfully. He should have chased them, dammit. Why hadn't he?

The heart was beating every three minutes now. The throat wound had closed, forming a large ridge under the dried blood. Cells multiplied at fantastic rates, spanning the damaged area with a minute latticework. This filled in as the new cells divided, ex-

panded, and divided again.

Lucas reached for his clipboard and flipped on the interior lights. He glanced into the trees once before he began filling in his report. A voice crackled on the radio, calling another car. His pen scratched haltingly across the paper.

The heart was returning to its normal pace. The ridge on the neck was gone, leaving smooth skin. A jagged pattern of light jerked across the retinas. The fugue was coming to an end. The chest rose, fell, then rose again. A shadow of awareness nudged at consciousness.

The sound of the radio filled the night again, and Lucas turned uneasily, searching the road behind him for approaching headlights. There were none. He glanced at his watch and then returned to the report.

She became aware of the familiar prickling sensation in her limbs, plus a strange burning about her throat. She felt herself rising, rising—and suddenly awareness flooded her. Her body jerked, uncurled. Jeanette opened her eyes. Breathing deeply, she blinked until the dark thick line looming over her resolved itself into a tree trunk. Unconsciously her hand began to rub her neck, and she felt dry flakes come off on her fingers.

Wearily she closed her eyes again, trying to remember: Those kids. One had a knife. She was in the park. Then she heard the faint crackle of a police radio. She rolled to her knees, and dizziness swept over her. She could see a light through the trees. Good God, she thought, he's right over there!

Jeanette rubbed her eyes and looked about her. She was lightheaded, but there was no time to waste. Soon there would be other police—and doctors. She knew. Moving unsteadily, at a crouch, she slipped away into the woods.

§ § §

Four patrol cars were there when the ambulance arrived. Stuart Crosby, the medical examiner, climbed out slowly and surveyed the scene. He could see half a dozen flashlights in the woods. The photographer sat in the open doorway of one of the cars, smoking a cigarette.

"Where's the body?" asked Crosby.

The photographer tossed his cigarette away disgustedly. "They can't find it."

"Can't find it? What do you mean?"

"It's not out there. Lucas says it was in the woods, but when Kelaney got here, it was gone."

Puzzled, Crosby turned toward the flashlights. As another gust of wind swept the park, he pulled his light coat more closely about him and started forward resignedly—a tired white-haired man who should have been home in bed.

He could hear Detective Kelaney roaring long before he could see him. "You half-ass! What'd it do, walk away?"

"No, sir!" answered Lucas hotly. "She was definitely dead. She was lying right there, I swear it—and that knife was in her throat, I recognize the handle."

"Yeah? For a throat wound, there's not much blood on it."

"Maybe," said Lucas stubbornly, "but that's where it was, all right."

Crosby halted. He had a moment of disorientation as uneasy memories stirred in the back of his mind. A serious wound, but not much blood . . . a dead body that disappeared . . .

"Obviously she wasn't dragged," said Kelany. "Did you by chance, *Officer* Lucas, think to check the pulse? Or were you thinking at all?"

"Yes, sir! Yes, I did! I checked the pulse, and there was nothing! Zero respiration, too. Yes, sir, I did!"

"Then where *is* she?" screamed Kelaney.

Another officer approached timidly. "There's nothing out there, sir. Nothing at all."

"Well, look again," snarled Kelaney.

Crosby moved into the circle of men. The detective was running his hand through his hair in exasperation. Lucas was red-faced and defiant.

Kelaney reached for his notebook. "All right, what did she look like?"

Lucas straightened, eager with facts. "Twenty, twenty-two, Caucasian, dark hair, about five-six, hundred and twenty-five pounds . . ."

"Scars or distinguishing marks?"

"Yeah, as a matter of fact. There were three moles on her cheek—on her left cheek—all right together, right about here." He put his finger high on his cheekbone, near his eye.

Crosby felt the blood roar in his ears. He stepped forward. "What did you say, Lucas?" he asked hoarsely.

Lucas turned to the old man. "Three moles, doctor, close together, on her cheek."

Crosby turned away, his hands in his pockets. He took a deep breath. He'd always known she'd return some day, and here was the same scene, the same bewildered faces, the same accusations. Three moles on her cheek . . . it had to be.

The wind ruffled his hair, but he no longer noticed its chill. They would find no body. Jeanette was back.

The next morning, Crosby filed a Missing Persons Report. "Send out an APB," he told the sergeant. "We've got to find her."

The sergeant looked mildly surprised. "What's she done?"

"She's a potential suicide. More than potential. I know this woman, and she's going to try to kill herself."

The sergeant reached for the form. "Okay, Doc, if you think it's that important. What's her name?"

Crosby hesitated. "She's probably using an alias. But I can give a description—an exact description."

"Okay," said the sergeant. "Shoot."

The bulletin went out at noon. Crosby spent the remainder of the day visiting motels, but no one remembered checking in a young woman with three moles on her cheek.

Jeanette saw the light approaching in the distance: two white eyes and, above them, the yellow and red points along the roof that told her this was a truck. She leaned back against the concrete support of the bridge, hands clenched behind her, and waited.

It had been three nights since the incident in the park. Her shoulders sagged dejectedly at the thought of it. Opportunities like that were everywhere, but she knew that knives weren't going to do it. She'd tried that herself—was it in Cleveland? A painful memory flashed for a moment, of one more failure in the long series of futile attempts—heartbreaking struggles in the wrong cities. But here—

She peered around the pillar again. The eyes of the truck were closer now. Here, it could happen. Where it began, it could end. She inched closer to the edge of the support and crouched, alert to the sound of the oncoming truck.

It had rounded the curve and was thundering down the long straightaway before the bridge. Joy surged within her as she grasped its immensity and momentum. Surely this . . . ! Never had she tried it with something so large, with something beyond her control. Yes, surely this would be the time!

Suddenly the white eyes were there, racing under the bridge, the diesels throbbing, roaring down at her. Her head reared in elation. Now!

She leaped an instant too late, and her body was struck by the right fender. The mammoth impact threw her a hundred feet in an arc that spanned the entrance ramp, the guideposts, and a ditch, terminating brutally in the field beyond. The left side of her skull was smashed, her arm was shattered, and four ribs were caved in. The impact of the landing broke her neck.

It was a full quarter of a mile before the white-faced driver gained sufficient control to lumber to a halt. "Sweet Jesus," he whispered. Had he imagined it? He climbed out of the rig and examined the dented fender. Then he ran back to the cab and tried futilely to contact someone by radio who could telephone the police. It was 3 AM, and all channels seemed dead. Desperately he began backing along the shoulder.

Rushes of energy danced through the tissues. Cells divided furiously, bridging gulfs. Enzymes flowed; catalysts swept through protoplasm: coupling, breaking, then coupling again. Massive reconstruction raged on. The collapsed half of the body shifted imperceptibly.

The truck stopped a hundred feet from the bridge, and the driver leaped out. He clicked on his flashlight and played it frantically over the triangle of thawing soil between the entrance ramp and the expressway. Nothing. He crossed to the ditch and began walking slowly beside it.

Bundles of collagen interlaced; in the matrix, mineral was deposited; cartilage calcified. The ribs had almost knit together and were curved loosely in their original crescent. Muscle fibers united and contracted in taut arches. The head jerked, then jerked again, as it was forced from its slackness into an increasingly firm position. Flexor spasms twitched the limbs as impulses flowed through newly formed neurons. The heart pulsed.

The driver stood helplessly on the shoulder and clicked off the flashlight. It was 3:30, and no cars were in sight. He couldn't find the body. He had finally succeeded in radioing for help, and now all he could do was wait. He stared at the ditch for a moment before moving toward the truck. There *had* been a woman, he was sure. He'd seen her for just an instant before the impact, leaping forward under the headlights. He shuddered and quickened his pace to the cab.

Under the caked blood, the skin was smooth and softly rounded. The heart was pumping her awake: Scratches of light behind the eyelids. Half of her body prickling, burning . . . A shuddering breath.

Forty-seven minutes after the impact, Jeanette opened her eyes. Slowly she raised her head. That line in the sky . . . the bridge.

She had failed again. Even here. She opened her mouth to moan, but only a rasping sound emerged.

Stuart Crosby swayed as the ambulance rounded a corner and sped down the street. He pressed his knuckles against his mouth and screamed silently at the driver: God, hurry, I know it's her.

He had slept little since the night in the park. He had monitored every call, and he knew that this one—a woman in dark clothes, jumping in front of a trucker's rig—this one had to be Jeanette.

It was her. She was trying again. Oh, God, after all these years, she was still trying. How many times, in how many cities, had she fought to die?

They were on the bridge now, and he looked down on the figures silhouetted against the red of the flares. The ambulance swung into the entrance ramp with a final whoop and pulled up behind a patrol car. Crosby had the door open and his foot on the ground before they were completely stopped, and he had to clutch at the door to keep from falling. A pain flashed across his back. He regained his balance and ran toward a deputy who was playing a flashlight along the ditch.

"Did you find her?"

The deputy turned and took an involuntary step

away from the intense, stooped figure. "No, sir, doctor. Not a thing."

Crosby's voice failed him. He stood looking dejectedly down the expressway.

"To tell you the truth," said the deputy, nodding at the semi, "I think that guy had a few too many little white pills. Seeing shadows. There's nothing along here but a dead raccoon. And he's been dead since yesterday."

But Crosby was already moving across the ditch to the field beyond, where deputies swung flashlights in large arcs and a German shepherd was snuffling through the brittle stubble.

Somewhere near here, Jeanette might be lying with a broken body. It was possible, he thought. The damage could have been great, and the healing slow. Or—a chill thought clutched at him. He shook his head. No. She wouldn't have succeeded. She would still be alive, somewhere. If he could just see her, talk to her!

There was a sharp, small bark from the dog. Crosby hurried forward frantically. His foot slipped and he came down hard, scraping skin from his palm. The pain flashed again in his back. He got to his feet and ran toward the circle of deputies.

One of the men was crouched, examining the cold soil. Crosby ran up, panting, and saw that the ground was stained with blood. She'd been here. She'd been here!

He strained to see across the field and finally discerned, on the other side, a road running parallel to the expressway. But there were no cars parked on it. She was gone.

After he returned home, his body forced him to sleep, but his dreams allowed him no rest. He kept seeing a lovely young woman, with three moles on her cheek—a weeping, haunted, frantic woman who cut herself again and again and thrust the mutilated arm before his face for him to watch in amazement as the wounds closed, bonded, and healed to smoothness before his eyes. In minutes.

God, if she would only stop crying, stop pleading with him, stop begging him to find a way to make her die—to use his medical knowledge somehow, in some manner that would end it for her. She wanted to die. She hated herself, hated the body that imprisoned her.

How old was she then? How many years had that youthful body endured without change, without aging? How many decades had she lived before life exhausted her and she longed for the tranquillity of death?

He had never found out. He refused to help her die, and she broke away and fled hysterically into the night. He never saw her again. There followed a series of futile suicide attempts and night crimes with the young woman victim mysteriously missing—and then . . . nothing.

And now she was back. Jeanette!

He found himself sitting up in bed, and he wearily buried his face in his hands. He could still hear the sound of her crying. He had always heard it, in a small corner of his mind, for the last thirty years.

The street sign letters were white on green: HOMER. Jeanette stood for a long while staring at them before she turned to walk slowly along the crumbling sidewalk. A vast ache filled her chest as she beheld the familiar old houses.

The small, neat lawns had been replaced by weeds and litter. Bricks were missing out of most of the front walks. The fence was gone at the Mahews'. Jim Mahew had been so proud the day he brought home his horseless carriage, and she'd been the only one brave enough to ride in it. Her mother had been horrified.

This rambling old home with the boarded up windows was the Parkers'. The house was dead now. So was her playmate, Billy Parker—the first boy she knew to fight overseas and the first one to die. The little house across the street had been white when old Emma Walters lived there. She had baked sugar cookies for Jeanette, and Jeanette had given her a May basket once, full of violets. She must have died a long time ago. Jeanette's hand clenched. A very long time ago.

The sound of her steps on the decayed sidewalk seemed extraordinarily loud. The street was deserted. There was no movement save that of her own dark figure plodding steadily forward. Here was Cathy Carter's house. Her father had owned the buggywhip factory over in Capville. They'd been best friends. Cathy, who always got her dresses dirty, had teeth missing, cut off her own braids one day. There was that Sunday they'd gotten in trouble for climbing the elm tree—but there was no elm now, only an ugly stump squatting there to remind her of a Sunday that was gone, lost, wiped out forever. She'd heard that Cathy had married a druggist and moved out East somewhere. Jeanette found herself wondering desperately if Cathy had raised any children. Or grandchildren. Or great-grandchildren. Cathy Carter, did you make your little girls wear dresses and braids? Did you let them climb trees? Are you still alive? Or are you gone, too, like everything else that ever meant anything to me?

Her steps faltered, but her own house loomed up ahead to draw her on. It stood waiting, silently watching her approach. It, too, was dead. A new pain filled her when she saw the crumbling porch, saw that the flowerboxes were gone, saw the broken windows and the peeling wallpaper within. A rusted bicycle wheel lay in the weeds that were the front yard, along with a box of rubble and pile of boards. Tiny pieces of glass crunched sharply beneath her feet. The hedge was gone. So were the boxwood shrubs, the new variety from Boston—her mother had waited for them for so long and finally got them after the war.

She closed her eyes. Her mother had never known. Had died before she realized what she had brought into the world. Before even Jeanette had an inkling of what she was.

A monster. A freak. This body was wrong, horribly wrong. It should not be.

She had run away from this town, left it so that her friends would never know. But still it pulled at her, drawing her back every generation, pushing itself into her thoughts until she could stand it no longer. Then she would come back to stare at the old places that had been her home and the old people who had been her friends. And they didn't recognize her, never suspected, never knew why she seemed so strangely familiar.

Once she had even believed she could live here again. The memory ached within her and she quickened her pace. She could not think of him, could not allow the sound of his name in her mind. Where was he now? Had he ever understood? She had run away that time, too.

She'd had to. He was so good, so generous, but she was grotesque, a vile caprice of nature. She loathed the body.

It was evil. It must be destroyed.

Here, in the city where it was created: Where she was born, she would die.

Somehow.

The phone jangled harshly, shattering the silence of the room with such intensity that he jumped and dropped a slide on the floor. He sighed and reached for the receiver. "Crosby."

"Doctor, this is Sergeant Anderson. One of our units spotted a woman fitting the description of your APB on the High Street Bridge."

"Did they get her?" demanded Crosby.

"I dunno yet. They just radioed in. She was over the railing—looked like she was ready to jump. They're trying to get to her now. Thought you'd like to know."

"Right," said Crosby, slamming down the receiver. He reached for his coat as his mind plotted out the fastest route to High Street. Better cut down Fourth, he thought, and up Putnam. The slide crackled sharply under his heel and he looked at it in brief surprise before running out the door.

They've found her, he thought elatedly. They've got Jeanette! Thank God—I must talk with her, must convince her that she's a miracle. She has the secret of life. The whole human race will be indebted to her. Please, please, he prayed, don't let her get away.

He reached the bridge and saw the squad car up ahead. Gawkers were driving by slowly, staring out of their windows in morbid fascination. Two boys on bicycles had stopped and were peering over the railing. An officer had straddled it and was looking down.

Crosby leaped from the car and ran anxiously to the railing. His heart lifted as he saw another officer, with one arm around the lower railing and a firm grip on Jeanette's wrist. He was coaxing her to take a step up.

"Jeanette!" It was a ragged cry.

"Take it easy, Doc," said the officer straddling the railing. "She's scared."

The woman looked up. She was pale, and the beauty mark on her cheek stood out starkly. The bitter shock sent Crosby reeling backward. For a moment he felt dizzy, and he clutched the rail with trembling fingers. The gray river flowed sullenly beneath him.

It wasn't Jeanette.

"Dear God," he whispered. He finally raised his gaze to the dismal buildings that loomed across the river. Then where was she? She must have tried again. Had she succeeded?

Chief Dolenz clasped, then unclasped his hands. "You've got to slow down, Stu. You're pushing yourself far too hard."

Crosby's shoulders sagged a little more, but he did not answer.

"You're like a man possessed," continued the Chief. "It's starting to wear you down. Ease up, for God's sake. We'll find her. Why all this fuss over one loony patient? Is it that important, really?"

Crosby lowered his head. He still couldn't speak. The Chief looked with puzzlement at the old man, at the small bald spot that was beginning to expand, at the slump of the body, the rumpled sweater, the tremor of the hands as they pressed together. He opened his mouth but could not bring himself to say more.

"Citizens National Bank," the switchboard operator said.

The voice on the line was low and nervous. "I'm gonna tell you this once, and only once. There's a bomb in your bank, see? It's gonna go off in ten minutes. If you don't want nobody hurt, you better get 'em outta there."

The operator felt the blood drain from her face. "Is this a joke?"

"No joke, lady. You got ten minutes. If anybody wants to know, you tell 'em People for a Free Society are starting to take action. Got that?" The line went dead.

She sat motionless for a moment, and then she got unsteadily to her feet. "Mrs. Calkins!" she called. The switchboard buzzed again, but she ignored it and ran to the manager's desk.

Mrs. Calkins looked up from a customer and frowned icily at her; but when the girl bent and whispered in her ear, the manager got calmly to her feet. "Mr. Davison," she said politely to her customer, "we seem to have a problem in the bank. I believe the safest place to be right now would be out of the building." Turning to the operator, she said coolly, "Notify the police."

Mr. Davison scrambled to his feet and began

thrusting papers into his briefcase. The manager strode to the center of the lobby and clapped her hands with authority. "Could I have your attention please! I'm the manager. We are experiencing difficulties in the bank. I would like everyone to move quickly but quietly out of the building and into the street. Please move some distance away."

Faces turned toward her, but no one moved.

"Please," urged Mrs. Calkins. "There is immediate danger if you remain in the building. Your transactions may be completed later. Please leave at once."

People began to drift toward the door. The tellers looked at each other in bewilderment and began locking the money drawers. A heavyset man remained stubbornly at his window. "What about my change?" he demanded.

The operator hung up the phone and ran toward the doorway. "Hurry!" she cried. "There's a bomb!"

"A bomb!"

"She said there's a bomb!"

"Look out!"

"Get outside!"

There was a sudden rush for the door. "Please!" shouted the manager. "There is no need for panic." But her voice was lost in the uproar.

Jeanette sat limply at the bus stop, her hands folded in her lap, her eyes fixed despondently on the blur of passing automobile wheels. The day was oppressively overcast; gray clouds hung heavily over the city. When the chill wind blew her coat open, she made no move to gather it about her.

Behind her, the doors of the bank suddenly burst open, and people began to rush out frantically. The crowd bulged into the street. Brakes squealed; voices babbled excitedly. Jeanette turned and looked dully toward the bank.

There were shouts. Passing pedestrians began to run, and the frenzied flow of people from the bank continued. A woman screamed. Another tripped and nearly fell. Sirens sounded in the distance.

Above the hubbub, Jeanette caught a few clearly spoken words. "Bomb . . . in the bank . . ." She got slowly to her feet and began to edge her way through the crowd.

She had almost reached the door before anyone tried to stop her. A man caught at her sleeve. "You can't go in there, lady. There's a bomb!"

She pulled free, and a fresh surge of pedestrians came between them. The bank doors were closed, now. Everyone was outside and hurrying away. Jeanette pushed doubtfully at the tall glass door, pushed it open further, and slipped inside. It closed with a hiss, blocking out the growing pandemonium in the street. The lobby seemed warm and friendly, a refuge from the bitterly cold wind.

She turned and looked through the door. A policeman had appeared and the man who had tried to stop her was talking with him and pointing at the bank. Jeanette quickly moved back out of sight. She walked the length of the empty room, picked out a chair for herself, and sat down. The vast, unruffled quiet of the place matched the abiding peace she felt within her.

Outside, the first police car screamed to the curb. An ambulance followed, as the explosion ripped through the building, sending a torrent of bricks and glass and metal onto the pavement.

"Code blue, emergency room." The loudspeaker croaked for the third time as Julius Beamer rounded the corner. Ahead of him he could see a woman being wheeled into room three. An intern, keeping pace with the cart, was pushing on her breastbone at one-second intervals.

Emergency room three was crowded. A nurse stepped aside as he entered and said, "Bomb exploded at the bank." A technician was hooking up the EKG, while a young doctor was forcing a tube down the woman's trachea. A resident had inserted an IV and called for digoxin.

"Okay," said Dr. Beamer to the intern thumping the chest. The intern stepped back, exhausted, and Beamer took over the external cardiac massage. The respirator hissed into life. Beamer pressed down.

There was interference. Excess oxygen was flooding the system. A brief hesitation, and then the body adjusted. Hormones flooded the bloodstream, and the cells began dividing again. The site of the damage was extensive, and vast reconstruction was necessary. The heart pulsed once.

There was a single blip on the EKG, and Beamer grunted. He pushed again. And then again, but the flat high-pitched note continued unchanged. Dr. Channing was at his elbow, waiting to take over, but Beamer ignored him. Julius Beamer did not like failure. He called for the electrodes. A brief burst of electricity flowed into the heart. There was no response. He applied them again.

The reconstruction was being hindered: there was cardiac interference. The body's energies were diverted toward the heart in an effort to keep it from beating. The delicate balance had to be maintained, or the chemicals would be swept away in the bloodstream.

A drop of sweat trickled down Julius Beamer's temple. He called for a needle and injected epinephrine directly into the heart.

Chemical stimulation: hormones activated and countered immediately.

There was no response. The only sounds in the room were the long hisssssss-click of the respirator and the eerie unchanging note of the EKG. Dr. Beamer stepped back wearily and shook his head. Then he whirled in disgust and strode out of the room. A resident reached to unplug the EKG.

The interference had stopped. Reconstruction resumed at the primary site of damage.

Rounding the corner, Dr. Beamer heard someone call his name hoarsely, and he turned to see Stuart Crosby stumbling toward him.

"Julius! That woman!"

"Stuart! Hello! What are you—?"

"That woman in the explosion. Where is she?"

"I'm afraid we lost her—couldn't get her heart going. Is she a witness?"

In emergency room three, the respirator hissed to a stop. *The heart pulsed once.* But there was no machine to record it.

In the hallway, Crosby clutched at Dr. Beamer. "No. She's my wife."

Crosby's fists covered his eyes, his knuckles pressing painfully into his forehead. Outside, there was a low rumble of thunder. He swallowed with difficulty and dug his knuckles in deeper, trying to reason. How can I? he wondered. How can I say yes? Jeanette!

The figure behind him moved slightly and the woman cleared her throat. "Dr. Crosby, I know this is a difficult decision, but we haven't much time." She laid a gentle hand on his shoulder. "We've got forty-three people in this area who desperately need a new kidney. And there are three potential recipients for a heart upstairs—one is an eight-year-old girl. Please. It's a chance for someone else. A whole new life."

Crosby twisted away from her and moved to the window. No, he thought, we haven't much time. In a few minutes, she would get up off that table herself and walk into this room—and then it would be too late. She wanted to die. She had been trying to die for years—how many? Fifty? A hundred? If they took her organs, she *would* die. Not even that marvelous body could sustain the loss of the major organs. All he had to do was say yes. But how could he? He hadn't even seen her face yet. He could touch her again, talk to her, hold her. After thirty years!

As he looked out the window, a drop of rain splashed against the pane. He thought of the lines of a poem he had memorized twenty years before.

From too much love of living,
　　From hope and fear set free,
We thank with brief thanksgiving
　　Whatever gods may be
That no man lives forever,
That dead men rise up never;
That even the weariest river
　　Winds somewhere safe to sea.

The rain began to fall steadily, drumming against the window in a hollow rhythm. There was silence in the room, and for a brief moment, Crosby had the frightening sensation of being totally alone in the world.

A voice within him spoke the painful answer: Release her. Let her carry the burden no more. She is weary.

"Dr. Crosby . . ." The woman's voice was gentle.

"Yes!" he cried. "Do it! Take everything—anything you want. But God, please hurry!" Then he lowered his head into his hands and wept.

Grafton Medical Center was highly efficient. Within minutes, a surgeon was summoned and preparations had begun. The first organs removed were the kidneys. Then the heart. Later, the liver, pancreas, spleen, eyeballs, and thyroid gland were lifted delicately and transferred to special containers just above freezing temperature. Finally, a quantity of bone marrow was removed for use as scaffolding for future production of peripheral blood cellular components.

What had been Jeanette Crosby was wheeled down to the morgue.

The woman's voice was doubtful. "We usually don't allow relatives. You see, once the services are over . . ."

Stuart Crosby clutched his hat. "There were no services. I only want a few minutes."

The owner of the crematory, a burly, pleasant looking man, entered the outer office. "Can I do something for you, sir?"

The woman turned to him. "He wanted a little time with the casket, Mr. Gilbert. The one that came over from the hospital this morning."

"Please," Crosby pleaded. "There were no services—I didn't want any, but I just—I didn't realize there'd be no chance to say good-bye. The hospital said she was sent here, and . . . I'm a doctor. Dr. Stuart Crosby. She's my wife. Jeanette Crosby. I didn't think until today that I wanted to . . ." He trailed off and lowered his head.

The owner hesitated. "We usually don't allow this, doctor. We have no facilities here for paying the last respects."

"I know," mumbled Crosby. "I understand—but just a few minutes—please."

The manager looked at the secretary, then back to the old man. "All right, sir. Just a moment, and I'll see if I can find a room. If you'll wait here, please."

The casket was cream-colored pine. It was unadorned. The lid was already sealed, so he could not see her face. But he knew it would be at peace.

He stood dry-eyed before the casket, his hands clasped in front of him. Outside, the rain that had begun the day before was still drizzling down. He could think of nothing to say to her, and he was only aware of a hollow feeling in his chest. He thought ramblingly of his dog, and how he hadn't made his bed that morning, and about the broken windshield wiper he would have to replace on his car.

Finally he turned and walked from the room, bent over a bit because his back hurt. "Thank you," he said to the owner. Stepping outside into the rain, he very carefully raised his umbrella.

The owner watched him until the car pulled onto the main road. Then he yelled, "Okay Jack!"

Two men lifted the casket and bore it outside in the rain toward the oven.

Cells divided, differentiated, and divided again. The reconstruction was almost complete. It had taken a long time, almost twenty-four hours. The body had never been challenged to capacity before. Removal of the major organs had caused much difficulty, but regeneration had begun almost at once, and the new tissues were now starting the first stirrings of renewed activity.

The casket slid onto the asbestos bricks with a small scraping noise. The door clanged shut, and there was a dull ring as the bolt was drawn.

There was a flicker of light behind the eyelids, and the new retinas registered it and transmittted it to the brain. The heart pulsed once, and then again. A shuddering breath.

Outside the oven, a hand reached for the switches and set the master timer. The main burner was turned on. Oil under pressure flared and exploded into the chamber.

There was a shadow of awareness for a long moment, and then it was gone.

After thirty minutes, the oven temperature was nine hundred degrees Fahrenheit. The thing on the table was a third of its original size. The secondary burners flamed on. In another half hour, the temperature had reached two thousand degrees, and it would stay there for another ninety minutes.

The ashes, larger than usual, had to be mashed to a chalky, brittle dust.

As Dr. Kornbluth began easing off the dressing, she smiled at the young face on the pillow before her.

"Well, well. You're looking perky today, Marie!" she said.

The little girl smiled back with surprising vigor.

"Scissors, please," said Dr. Kornbluth and held out her hand.

Dr. Roeber spoke from the other side of the bed. "Her color is certainly good."

"Yes. I just got the lab report, and so far there's no

anemia."

"Has she been given the Prednisone today?"

"Twenty milligrams about an hour ago."

The last dressing was removed, and the two doctors bent over to examine the chest: the chest that was smooth and clean and faintly pink, with no scars, no lumps, no ridges.

"Something's wrong." said Dr. Korbluth. "Is this a joke, Dr. Roeber?"

The surgeon's voice was frightened. "I don't understand it, not at all."

"Have you the right patient here?" She reached for the identification bracelet around Marie's wrist.

"Of course it's the right patient!" Dr. Roeber's voice rose. "I ought to know who I operated on, shouldn't I?"

"But it isn't possible!" cried Dr. Kornbluth.

The girl spoke up in a high voice. "Is my new heart okay?"

"It's fine, honey," said Dr. Kornbluth. Then she lowered her voice. "This is physiologically impossible! The incision has completely healed, without scar tissue. And in thirty-two hours, doctor? In thirty-two hours?"

ON THE MARTIAN PROBLEM
by Randall Garrett

I am not at liberty to reveal whence I obtained the Xerox copy of this letter, nor why it was specifically sent to me rather than, say, Mr. Philip José Farmer, who would be far more qualified than I for the honor of putting it before the public. My duty, however, was clear, and with the kind co-operation of Dr. Isaac Asimov and Mr. George Scithers, it is herewith submitted for your perusal. The letter itself is written in a bold, highly legible, masculine hand. The heading shows that it was written in Richmond, Virginia, and it is addressed to a numbered postal box in Nairobi. The bracketed notes after certain of the writer's expressions were added by myself.

My dear Ed,

Since your secret retirement to Africa, we have had much less communication than I would like; but, alas, my duties at home have kept me busy these many years. It is, however, a comfort to know that, thanks to the Duke's special serum, you will, barring accident or assassination, be around as long as I.

I am sorry not to have answered your last letter sooner, but, truth to tell, it caused me a great deal of consternation. I fear I had not been keeping up with the affairs of Earth as much as I perhaps should have, and I had no idea that the Mariner and Viking spacecraft had sent back such peculiar data.

One sentence in your last letter made me very proud: "I would rather believe that every man connected with NASA and JPL is a liar and a hoaxer than to believe you would ever tell me a deliberate lie." But, as you say, those photographs are most convincing.

Naturally, I took the photoreproductions you sent to a group of the wisest savants of Helium, and bade them do their best to solve the problem. They strove mightily, knowing my honor was at stake. Long they pondered over the data, and, with a science that is older and more advanced than that of Earth, they came up with an answer.

The tome they produced is far longer and far heavier than any book you have ever published, and is filled with page after page of abstruse mathematics, all using Martian symbolism. I could not translate it for you if I wished.

In fact, I had to get old Menz Klausa to explain it to me. He is not only learned in Martian mathematics, but has the knack of making things understandable to one who is not as learned as he. I shall endeavor to make the whole thing as clear to you as he made it to me.

First, you must consider in greater detail the method I use in going to Mars. There are limitations in time, for one thing. Mars must be almost directly overhead, and it must be about midnight. To use modern parlance, my "window" is small.

At such times, Mars is about 1.31×10^6 *karads* [4.88×10^7 miles] from Earth.

I call your attention to my description of what happens when I gaze up at the planet of the War God. I must focus my attention upon it strongly. Then I must bring to the fore an emotion which I can best describe as *yearning*. A moment's spark of cold and dark, and I find myself on Mars.

There is no doubt in my mind that I actually travel *through* that awful stretch of interplanetary void. It is *not* instantaneous; it definitely requires a finite time.

And yet, for all that I travel through nearly fifty million miles of hard vacuum naked, or nearly so, I suffer no effects of explosive decompression, no lack of breath, no popping of the eardrums, no nosebleed, no "hangover" eyeballs.

Obviously, then, I am exposed to those extreme conditions *for so short a time that my body does not have the time to react to them!*

Consider, also, that the distance is such that light requires some 296 *tals* [262 seconds] to make the trip. Had I been in the void that long, I would surely have been dead on arrival. Quite obviously, then, when I make such trips, *I am traveling faster than light!*

There is, unfortunately, no way of telling *how* much faster, for I have no way of timing it, but Menz Klausa is of the opinion that it is many multiples of that velocity.

Now we must consider what is known to Earth science as the "time dilation factor." I must translate from Martian symbols, but I believe it may be expressed as:

$$T_v = T_0[1-(v^2/c^2)]^{1/2}$$

where T_v is time lapse at velocity v, T_0 is the time lapse at rest, v is the velocity of the moving body, and c is the velocity of light.

The Martians, however, multiply this by another factor:

$$[(c-v)/(c^2-2cv+v^2)^{1/2}]^{1/2}$$

Thus, the entire equation becomes:

$$T_v = T_0[1-(v^2/c^2)]^{1/2} [(c-v)/(c^2-2cv+v^2)^{1/2}]^{1/2}$$

As you can clearly see, as long as the velocity of the moving body remains below the velocity of light (443,778 *haads* per *tal*), the first factor is a positive number, and the second factor has a value of +1. This, I believe, is why it has never been discovered by Earth scientists; multiplying a number by +1 has no effect whatever, and is not noticeable.

When v is exactly equal to c, both factors become

zero; in other words, the moving body experiences zero time. Its clock stops, so to speak.

However, when v exceeds c, the equation assumes the form:

$$T_v = T_0(xi) \, (i)$$

where i is the square root of minus one, and x is a function of v.

If the second, or Martian, factor is neglected, it is obvious that the experienced time of the moving body would become imaginary, which is unimaginable in our universe.

However:

$$(xi) \, (i) = xi^2 = -x$$

In other words, if the body is moving at greater than the velocity of light, the elapsed time becomes negative. *The body is moving backwards in time!*

According to the most learned savants in Helium, this is exactly what happened to me. Indeed, so great was my velocity that I traveled an estimated 50,000 years into the past!

Thus, the Mars that I am used to has, in Earth terms, been dead for fifty millennia.

This explanation seemed perfectly sound when Menz Klausa first elucidated it, but suddenly a thought occurred to me.

Why did I always go forward *in time when I returned to Earth?*

For surely that must be so, else I could not be here today. If that formula I quoted were complete, when I returned the first time, I should have found myself a hundred thousand years in the past, in about the year 98,000 B.C. Considering the number of trips I have made, I should, by now, be somewhere back in the Miocene.

However, that, too, is explained by our Martian theorists. Another factor comes into play at ultralight velocities, that of gravitation field strength. At light velocity, this factor accounts for the gravitational red-shift of light when it is attempting to escape from a strong gravitational field, and the violet-shift when the light is falling toward the gravity source.

At velocities greater than that of light, the factor becomes +1 when the direction of travel is from a greater gravitation field force to a lesser one, and −1 when the direction is from a lesser to a greater. Thus, when I return to Earth, the negative time factor becomes positive, and I go into the "future" of Mars, which is your "present."

I trust that is all very clear.

Unfortunately, there is no way I can translate the gravity factor into Earth's mathematical symbolism. I can handle simple algebra, but tensor calculus is a bit much. I am a fighting man, not a scientist.

By the way, it becomes obvious from this that the Gridley Wave is an ultralight and trans-time communicator.

Another puzzle that the photos brought out was that they show no trace of the canals of Mars. And yet, Giovanni Schiaparelli saw them. Percival Lowell not only saw them, but drew fairly accurate maps of them. I can testify to that, myself. And yet they do not show on the photographs taken from a thousand miles away. Why?

The answer is simple. As you know, certain markings that are quite unnoticeable from the ground are easily seen from the air. An aerial photograph can show the San Andreas Fault in California quite clearly, even in places where it is invisible from the ground. The same is true of ancient meteor craters which have long since weathered smooth, but have nonetheless left their mark on the Earth's surface. From an orbiting satellite, more markings become visible when there is a break in the cloud cover.

Many modern paintings must be viewed from a distance to understand the effect the artist wished to give. Viewed under a powerful magnifying glass, a newspaper photo becomes nothing but a cluster of meaningless dots. One is too close to get the proper perspective.

Thus it is with the canals of Mars, long since eroded away, from your viewpoint in time. In order to see those ancient markings properly, you have to stand back forty or fifty million miles.

But what is going to happen to the Mars I love? Or, from Earth's view point, what *did* happen to it?

According to Menz Klausa, that is explained by one significant feature on the photos you sent.

Remember, even "today" (from the Martian viewpoint), Mars is a dying planet. Our seas have long since vanished; our atmosphere is kept breathable only by our highly complex atmosphere plant. Martians have long since learned to face death stoically, even the death of the planet. We can face the catastrophe that will eventually overtake us.

From Earth's viewpoint in time, it happened some forty thousand years ago. A great mountain of rock from the Asteroid Belt—or perhaps from beyond the Solar System itself—came crashing into Mars at some 24 *haads* per *tal* [10 miles per second]. So great was its momentum that it smashed through the planetary crust to the magma beneath.

The resulting explosion wrought unimaginable havoc upon the planet—superheated winds of great velocity raced around the globe; great quakes shook the very bedrock; more of the atmosphere was literally blown into space, irretrievably lost.

But it left no impact crater like those of the Moon. The magma, hot and fluid, rushed up to form the mightiest volcano in the Solar System: Olympus Mons.

And the damned thing landed directly on our atmosphere plant!

However, we won't have to worry about that for another ten thousand years yet. Perhaps I won't live that long.

Give my best regards to Greystoke. Your Aunt Dejah sends her love.

All my best,
Uncle Jack

THE MISSING ITEM
by Isaac Asimov

Dr. Asimov's tales of the Black Widowers usually appear in Ellery Queen's Mystery Magazine; *it's a pleasure to borrow the Black Widowers for this issue of* IA'sf. *The real-life model for this little group includes among its membership L. Sprague de Camp and Martin Gardner, who appear elsewhere in this issue, Don Bensen, who illustrated this episode, your Editor, and of course Dr. Asimov himself. The real group—alas!—has no counterpart to the waiter, Henry, who is wholly fictional.*

Emmanuel Rubin, resident polymath of the Black Widowers Society, was visibly chafed. His eyebrows hunched down into the upper portion of his thick-lensed spectacles and his sparse gray beard bristled.

"Not true to life," he said. "Imagine! Not true to life!"

Mario Gonzalo, who had just reached the head of the stairs and had accepted his dry martini from Henry, the unsurpassable waiter, said, "What's not true to life?"

Geoffrey Avalon looked down from his seventy-four inches and said solemnly, "It appears that Manny has suffered a rejection."

"Well, why not?" said Gonzalo, peeling off his gloves. "Editors don't have to be stupid all the time."

"It isn't the rejection," said Rubin. "I've been rejected before by better editors and in connection with better stories. It's the reason he advanced! How the hell would he know if a story were true to life or not? What's he ever done but warm an office chair? Would he—"

Roger Halsted, whose career as a math teacher in

a junior high school had taught him how to interrupt shrill voices, managed to interpose. "Just what did he find not true to life, Manny?"

Rubin waved a hand passionately outward, "I don't want to talk about it."

"Good," said Thomas Trumbull, scowling from under his neatly-waved thatch of white hair. "Then the rest of us can hear each other for a while. —Roger, why don't you introduce your guest to the late Mr. Gonzalo?"

Halsted said, "I've just been waiting for the decibel-level to decrease. Mario, my friend Jonathan Thatcher. This is Mario Gonzalo, who is an artist by profession. Jonathan is an oboist, Mario."

Gonzalo grinned and said, "Sounds like fun."

"Sometimes it almost is," said Thatcher, "on days when the reed behaves itself."

Thatcher's round face and plump cheeks would have made him a natural to play Santa Claus at any Christmas benefit, but he would have needed padding just the same, for his body had that peculiar ersatz slimness that seemed to indicate forty pounds recently lost. His eyebrows were dark and thick and one took it for granted that they were never drawn together in anger.

Henry said, "Gentlemen, dinner is ready."

James Drake stubbed out his cigarette and said, "Thanks, Henry. It's a cold day and I would welcome hot food."

"Yes, sir," said Henry with a gentle smile. "Lobster thermidor today, baked potatoes, stuffed eggplant—"

"But what's this, Henry?" demanded Rubin, scowling.

"Hot borscht, Mr. Rubin."

Rubin looked as though he were searching his soul and then he said, grudgingly, "All right."

Drake, unfolding his napkin, said, "Point of order, Roger."

"What is it?"

"I'm sitting next to Manny, and if he continues to

113

look like that he'll curdle my soup and give me indigestion. You're host and absolute monarch; I move you direct him to tell us what he wrote that isn't true to life and get it out of his system."

"Why?" said Trumbull. "Why not let him sulk and be silent for the novelty of it?"

"I'm curious, too," said Gonzalo, "since nothing he's ever written has been true to life—"

"How would you know, since you can't read?" said Rubin, suddenly.

"It's generally known," said Gonzalo. "You hear it everywhere."

"Oh, God, I'd better tell you and end this miasma of pseudo-wit. —Look, I've written a novelette, about 15,000 words long, about a world-wide organization of locksmiths—"

"Locksmiths?" said Avalon, frowning as though he suspected he had not heard correctly.

"Locksmiths," said Rubin. "These guys are experts, they can open anything—safes, vaults, prison doors. There are no secrets from them and nothing can be hidden from them. My global organization is of the cream of the profession and no man can join the organization without some document or object of importance stolen from an industrial, political, or governmental unit.

"Naturally, they have the throat of the world in their grip. They can control the stock market, guide diplomacy, make and unmake governments, and—at the time my story opens—they are headed by a dangerous megalomaniac—"

Drake interrupted even as he winced in his effort to crack the claw of the lobster. "Who is out to rule the world, of course."

"Of course," said Rubin, "and our hero must stop him. He is himself a skilled locksmith—"

Trumbull interrupted. "In the first place, Manny, what the hell do you know about locksmithery or locksmithmanship or whatever you call it?"

"More than you think," retorted Rubin.

"I doubt that very much," said Trumbull, "and the editor is right. This is utter and complete implausibility. I know a few locksmiths and they're gentle and inoffensive mechanics with IQ's—"

Rubin said, "And I suppose when you were in the army you knew a few corporals and, on the basis of your knowledge, you'll tell me that Napoleon and Hitler were implausible."

The guest for that evening, who had listened to the exchange with a darkening expression, spoke up. "Pardon me, gentlemen, I know I'm to be grilled at the conclusion of dinner. Does that mean I cannot join the dinner conversation beforehand?"

"Heavens, no," said Halsted. "Talk all you want—if you can get a word in now and then."

"In that case, let me put myself forcefully on the side of Mr. Rubin. A conspiracy of locksmiths may sound implausible to us who sit here, but what counts is not what a few rational people think but what the great outside world does. How can your editor turn down anything at all as implausible when everything—" He caught himself, took a deep breath and said, in an altered tone, "Well, I don't mean to tell you your business. I'm not a writer. After all, I don't expect you to tell me how to play the oboe," but his smile as he said it was a weak one.

"Manny will tell you how to play the oboe," said Gonzalo, "if you give him a chance."

"Still," Thatcher said, as though he had not heard Gonzalo's comment, "I live in the world and observe it. *Anything* these days is believed. There is no such thing as 'not true to life'. Just spout any nonsense solemnly and swear it's true and there will be millions rallying round you."

Avalon nodded magisterially and said, "Quite right, Mr. Thatcher. I don't know that this is simply characteristic of our times, but the fact that we have better communications now makes it easier to reach many people quickly so that a phenomenon such as Herr Hitler of unmourned memory is possible. And to those who can believe in Mr. von Däniken's ancient astronauts and in Mr. Berlitz's Bermuda triangle, a little thing like a conspiracy of locksmiths could be swallowed with the morning porridge."

Thatcher waved his hand, "Ancient astronauts and Bermuda triangles are nothing. Suppose you were to say that you frequently visited Mars in astral projection and that Mars was, in fact, a haven for the worthy souls of this world. There would be those who would believe you."

"I imagine so," began Avalon.

"You don't have to imagine," said Thatcher. "It *is* so. I take it you haven't heard of Tri-Lucifer. That's T-R-I."

"Tri-Lucifer?" said Halsted, looking a little dumbfounded. "You mean three Lucifers. What's that?"

Thatcher looked from one face to another and the Black Widowers all remained silent.

And then Henry, who was clearing away some of the lobster shells, said, "If I may be permitted, gentlemen, I have heard of it. There was a group of them soliciting contributions at this restaurant last week."

"Like the Moonies?" said Drake, pushing his dish in Henry's direction and preparing to light up.

"There is a resemblance," said Henry, his unlined, sixtyish face a bit thoughtful, "but the Tri-Luciferians, if that is the term to use, give a more other-worldly appearance."

"That's right," said Thatcher. "They have to divorce themselves from this world so as to achieve astral projection to Mars and facilitate the transfer of their souls there after death."

"But why—" began Gonzalo.

And Trumbull suddenly roared out with a blast of anger. "Come on, Roger, make them wait for the grilling to start. Change the subject."

Gonzalo said, "I just want to know why they call them—"

116

Halsted sighed and said, "Let's wait a while, Mario."

§ § §

Henry was making his way about the table with the brandy when Halsted tapped his water glass and said, "I think we can begin the grilling now; and Manny, since it was your remark about true-to-lifeness that roused Jonathan's interest over the main course, why don't you begin."

"Sure." Rubin looked solemnly across the table at Thatcher and said, "Mr. Thatcher, at this point it would be traditional to ask you how you justify your existence and we would then go into a discussion of the oboe as an instrument of torture for oboists. *But,* let me guess and say that at this moment you would consider your life justified if you could wipe out a few Tri-Luciferians. Am I right?"

"You are, you are," said Thatcher, energetically. "The whole thing has filled my life and my thoughts for over a month now. It is ruining—"

Gonzalo interrupted. "What I want to know is why they call themselves Tri-Luciferians. Are they devil-worshipers or what?"

Rubin began, "You're interrupting the man—"

"It's all right," said Thatcher. "I'll tell him. I'm just sorry that I know enough about that organization to be able to tell him. Apparently, Lucifer means the morning star, though I'm not sure why—"

"Lucifer," said Avalon, running his finger about the lip of his water-glass, "is from Latin words meaning 'light-bringer'. The rising of the morning star in the dawn heralds the soon-following rising of the Sun. In an era in which there were no clocks that was an important piece of information to anyone awake at the time."

"Then why is Lucifer the name of the devil?" asked Gonzalo.

Avalon said, "Because the Babylonian king was apparently referred to as the Morning Star by his flattering courtiers, and the Prophet Isaiah predicted his destruction. Can you quote the passage, Manny?"

Rubin said, "We can read it out of the Bible, if we want to. It's the 14th Chapter of Isaiah. The key sentence goes, 'How art thou fallen from heaven, O Lucifer, son of the morning!' It was just a bit of poetic hyperbole, and very effective too, but it was interpreted literally later, and that one sentence gave rise to the whole myth of a rebellion against God by hordes of angels under the leadership of Lucifer, which came to be considered Satan's name while still in heaven. Of course, the rebels were defeated and expelled from heaven by loyalist angels under the leadership of the Archangel Michael."

"Like in *Paradise Lost*?" said Gonzalo.

"Exactly like in *Paradise Lost*."

Thatcher said, "The devil isn't part of it, though. To the Tri-Luciferians, Lucifer just means the morning star. There are two of them on Earth: Venus and Mercury."

Drake squinted through the curling tobacco smoke and said, "They're also evening stars, depending on which side of the Sun they happen to be. They're either east of the Sun and set shortly after Sunset, or west of the Sun and rise shortly before Sunrise."

Thatcher said, with clear evidence of hope, "Do they have to be both together; both one or both the other?"

"No," said Drake, "they move independently. They can be both evening stars, or both morning stars, or one can be an evening star and one a morning star. Or one or the other or both can be nearly in a line with the Sun and be invisible altogether, morning or evening."

"Too bad," said Thatcher, shaking his head, "that's what *they* say. —Anyway, the point is that from Mars you see *three* morning stars in the sky, or you can see them if they're in the right position: not only Mercury and Venus, but Earth as well."

"That's right," said Rubin.

"And," said Thatcher, "I suppose then it's true that

they can be in any position. They can all be evening stars or all morning stars, or two can be one and one can be the other?"

"Yes," said Drake, "Or one or more can be too close to the Sun to be visible."

Thatcher sighed. "So they call Mars by their mystic name of Tri-Lucifer—the world with the three morning stars."

"I suppose," said Gonzalo, "that Jupiter would have four morning stars: Mercury, Venus, Earth, and Mars; and so on out to Pluto, which would have eight morning stars."

"The trouble is," said Halsted, "that the farther out you go, the dimmer the inner planets are. Viewed from one of the satellites of Jupiter, for instance, I doubt that Mercury would appear more than a medium-bright star; and it might be too close to the Sun for anyone ever to get a good look at it."

"What about the view from Mars? Could you see Mercury?" asked Thatcher.

"Oh yes, I'm sure of that," said Halsted, "I could work out what the brightness would be in a matter of minutes."

"Would you?" said Thatcher.

"Sure," said Halsted, "if I've remembered to bring my pocket computer. —Yes, I have it. Henry, bring me the *Columbia Encyclopedia*, would you?"

Rubin said, "While Roger is bending his limited mathematical mind to the problem, Mr. Thatcher, tell us what your interest is in all this. You seem to be interested in exposing them as fakers. Why? Have you been a member? Are you now disillusioned?"

"No, I've never been a member. I—" He rubbed his temple hesitantly. "It's my wife. I don't like talking about it, you understand."

Avalon said solemnly, "Please be assured, Mr. Thatcher, that whatever is said here never passes beyond the bounds of this room. That includes our valued waiter, Henry. You may speak freely."

"Well, there's nothing criminal or disgraceful in it.

I just don't like to seem to be so helpless in such a silly— It's breaking up my marriage, gentlemen."

There was a discreet silence around the table, broken only by the mild sound of Halsted turning the pages of the encyclopedia.

Thatcher went on, "Roger knows my wife. He'll tell you she's a sensible woman—"

Halsted looked up briefly and nodded, "I'll vouch for that, but I didn't know you were having this—"

"Lately, Carol has not been social, you understand; and I certainly haven't talked about it. It was with great difficulty, you know, that I managed to agree to come out tonight. I dread leaving her to herself. You see, even sensible people have their weaknesses. Carol worries about death."

"So do we all," said Drake.

"So do I," said Thatcher, "But in a normal way, I hope. We all know we'll die someday and we don't particularly look forward to it, and we may worry about hell or nothingness or hope for heaven, but we don't think about it much. Carol has been fascinated, however, by the possibility of demonstrating the actual existence of life after death. It may have all started with the Bridey Murphy case when she was a teenager—I don't know if any of you remember that—"

"I do," said Rubin, "a woman under hypnosis seemed to be possessed by an Irishwoman who had died a long time before."

"Yes," said Thatcher. "She saw through that, eventually. Then she grew interested in spiritualism and gave that up. I always relied on her to understand folly when she finally stopped to think about it—and then she came up against the Tri-Luciferians. I never saw her like this. She wants to join them. She has money of her own and she wants to give it to them. I don't care about the money—well, I do, but that's not the main thing—I care about *her*. You know, she's going to join them in their retreat somewhere, become a daughter of Tri-Lucifer, or whatever they call it, and wait for translation to the Abode of the Blessed. One of these days, she'll be gone. I just won't see her anymore. She promised me it wouldn't be tonight, but I wonder."

Rubin said, "I take it you suppose that the organization is just interested in her money."

"At least the leader of it is," said Thatcher, grimly. "I'm sure of it. What else can he be after?"

"Do you know him? Have you met him?" said Rubin.

"No. He keeps himself isolated," said Thatcher, "but I hear he has recently bought a fancy mansion in Florida, and I doubt that it's for the use of the membership."

"Funny thing about that," said Drake. "It doesn't matter how lavishly a cult-leader lives, how extravagantly he throws money around. The followers, who support him and see their money clearly used for that purpose, never seem to mind."

"They identify," said Rubin. "The more he spends, the more successful they consider the cause. It's the basis of ostentatious waste in governmental display, too."

"Just the same," said Thatcher, "I don't think Carol will ever commit herself entirely. She might not be bothered by the leader's actions, but if I can prove him *wrong*, she'll drop it."

"Wrong about what?" asked Rubin.

"Wrong about Mars. This head of the group claims he has been on Mars often—in astral projection, of course. He describes Mars in detail, but can he be describing it accurately?"

"Why not?" asked Rubin. "If he reads up on what is known about Mars, he can describe it as astronomers would. The Viking photographs even show a part of the surface in detail. It's not difficult to be accurate."

"Yes, but it may be that somewhere he has made a mistake, something I can show Carol."

Halsted looked up and said, "Here, I've worked out

121

the dozen brightest objects in the Martian sky, together with their magnitudes. I may be off a little here and there, but not by much." He passed a slip of paper around.

Mario held up the paper when it reached him. "Would you like to see it, Henry?"

"Thank you, sir," murmured Henry, and as he glanced at it briefly, one eyebrow raised itself just slightly, just briefly.

The paper came to rest before Thatcher eventually and he gazed at it earnestly. What he saw was this:

Sun	−26.
Phobos	−9.6
Deimos	−5.1
Earth	−4.5
Jupiter	−3.1
Venus	−2.6
Sirius	−1.4
Saturn	−0.8
Canopus	−0.7
Alpha Centauri	−0.3
Arcturus	−0.1
Mercury	0.0

Thatcher said, "Phobos and Deimos are the two satellites of Mars. Do these numbers mean they're very bright?"

"The greater the negative number," said Halsted, "the brighter the object. A −2 object is two and a half times brighter than a −1 object and a −3 object is two and a half times brighter still and so on. Next to the Sun, Phobos is the brightest object in the Martian sky, and Deimos is next."

"And next to the Sun and the two satellites, Earth is the brightest object in the sky, then."

"Yes, but only at or near its maximum brightness," said Halsted. "It can be much dimmer depending on where Mars and Earth are in their respective orbits. Most of the time it's probably less bright than Jupiter, which doesn't change much in brightness as it moves in its orbit."

Thatcher shook his head and looked disappointed, "But it *can* be that bright. Too bad. There's a special prayer or psalm or something that the Tri-Luciferians have that appears in almost all their literature. I've seen it so often in the stuff Carol brings home, I can quote it exactly. It goes, 'When Earth shines high in the sky, like a glorious jewel, and when the other Lucifers have fled beyond the horizon, so that Earth shines alone in splendor, single in beauty, unmatched in brightness, it is then that the souls of those ready to receive the call must prepare to rise from Earth and cross the gulf.' And what you're saying, Roger, is that Earth *can* be the brightest object in the Martian sky."

Halsted nodded. "At night, if Phobos and Deimos are below the horizon, and Earth is near maximum brightness, it is certainly the brightest object in the sky. It would be three and a half times as bright as Jupiter, if that were in the sky, and six times as bright as Venus at its brightest."

"And it could be the only morning star in the sky."

"Or the only evening star. Sure. The other two, Venus and Mercury, could be on the other side of the Sun from Earth."

Thatcher kept staring at the list. "But would Mercury be visible? It's at the bottom of the list."

Halsted said, "The bottom just means that it's twelfth brightest, but there are thousands of stars that are dimmer and still visible. There would be only four stars brighter than Mercury as seen from Mars: Sirius, Canopus, Alpha Centauri, and Arcturus."

Thatcher said, "If they'd only make a mistake."

Avalon said in a grave and somewhat hesitant baritone, "Mr Thatcher, I think perhaps you had better face the facts. It is my experience that even if you *do* find a flaw in the thesis of the Tri-Luciferians it won't help you. Those who follow cults for emotional reasons are not deterred by demonstrations of the illogic of what they are doing."

Thatcher said, "I agree with you, and I wouldn't dream of arguing with the ordinary cultist. But I know Carol. I have seen her turn away from a system of beliefs she would very much like to have followed, simply because she saw the illogic of it. If I could find something of the sort here, I'm sure she'd come back."

Gonzalo said, "Some of us here ought to think of something. After all, he's never *really* been on Mars. He's got to have made a mistake."

"Not at all," said Avalon. "He probably knows as much about Mars as we do. Therefore, even if he's made a mistake it may be because he fails to understand something we also fail to understand and we won't catch him."

Thatcher nodded his head. "I suppose you're right."

"I don't know," said Gonzalo. "How about the canals? The Tri-Luciferians are bound to talk about the canals. Everyone believed in them and then just lately we found out they weren't there; isn't that right? So if he talks about them, he's caught."

Drake said, "Not everybody believed in them, Mario. Hardly any astronomers did."

"The general public did," said Gonzalo.

Rubin said, "Not lately. It was in 1964 that Mariner 4 took the first pictures of Mars and that pretty much gave away the fact the canals didn't exist. Once Mariner 9 mapped the whole planet in 1969 there was no further argument. When did the Tri-Luciferians come into existence, Mr. Thatcher?"

"As I recall," said Thatcher, "about 1970. Maybe 1971."

"There you are," said Rubin. "Once we had Mars down cold, this guy, whoever he is who runs it, decided to start a new religion based on it. Listen, if you want to get rich quick, no questions asked, start a new religion. Between the First Amendment and the tax breaks you get, it amounts to a license to help yourself to everything in sight. —I'll bet he talks about volcanoes."

Thatcher nodded. "The Martian headquarters of the astral projections are in Olympus Mons. That means Mount Olympus and that's where the souls of the righteous gather. That's the big volcano, isn't it?"

"The biggest in the Solar system," said Rubin. "At least, that we know of. It's been known since 1969."

Thatcher said, "The Tri-Luciferians say that G. V. Schiaparelli—he's the one who named the different places on Mars—was astrally inspired to name that spot Olympus to signify it was the home of the godly. In ancient Greece, you see, Mount Olympus was—"

"Yes," said Avalon, nodding gravely, "we know."

"Isn't Schiaparelli the fellow who first reported the canals?" asked Gonzalo.

"Yes," said Halsted, "although actually when he said 'canali' he meant natural waterways."

"Even so, why didn't the same astral inspiration tell him the canals weren't there?" asked Gonzalo.

Drake nodded and said, "That's something you can point out to your wife."

"No," said Thatcher, "I guess they thought of that. They say the canals were part of the inspiration because that increased interest in Mars and that that was needed to make the astral projection process more effective."

Trumbull, who had maintained a sullen silence through the discussion, as though he were waiting his chance to shift the discussion to oboes, said suddenly, "That makes a diseased kind of sense."

Thatcher said, "Too much makes sense. That's the trouble. There are times when I want to find a mistake not so much to save Carol as to save myself. I tell you that when I listen to Carol talking there's sometimes more danger she'll argue me into being crazy than that I'll persuade her to be rational."

Trumbull waved a hand at him soothingly, "Just take it easy and let's think it out. Do they say anything about the satellites?"

"They talk about them, yes. Phobos and Deimos. Sure."

"Do they say anything about how they cross the sky?" Trumbull's smile was nearly a smirk.

"Yes," said Thatcher, "and I looked it up because I didn't believe them and I thought I had something. In their description of the Martian scene, they talk about Phobos rising in the west and setting in the east. And it turns out that's true. And they say that whenever either Phobos or Deimos cross the sky at night, they are eclipsed by Mars's shadow for part of the time. And that's true, too."

Halsted shrugged. "The satellites were discovered a century ago, in 1877, by Asaph Hall. As soon as their distance from Mars and their period of revolution was determined, which was almost at once, their behavior in Mars's sky was known."

"*I* didn't know it," said Thatcher.

"No," said Halsted, "but this fellow who started the religion apparently did his homework. It wasn't really hard."

"Hold on," said Trumbull, truculently. "Some things aren't as obvious and don't get put into the average elementary astronomy textbook. For instance, I read somewhere that Phobos can't be seen from the Martian polar regions. It's so close to Mars that the bulge of Mars's spherical surface hides the satellite, if you go far enough north or south. Do the Tri-Luciferians say anything about Phobos being invisible from certain places on Mars, Thatcher?"

"Not that I recall," said Thatcher, "but they don't say it's always visible. If they just don't mention the matter, what does that prove?"

"Besides," said Halsted, "Olympus Mons is less than 20 degrees north of the Martian equator and Phobos is certainly visible from there any time it is above the horizon and not in eclipse. And if that's the headquarters for the souls from Earth, Mars would certainly be described as viewed from that place."

"Whose side are you on?" grumbled Trumbull.

"The truth's," said Halsted. "Still, it's true that astronomy books rarely describe any sky but Earth's. That's why I had to figure out the brightness of objects in the Martian sky instead of just looking it up. The only trouble is that this cult-leader seems to be just as good at figuring."

"I've got an idea," said Avalon. "I'm not much of an astronomer, but I've seen the photographs taken by the Viking landers, and I've read the newspaper reports about them. For one thing the Martian sky in the daytime is pink, because of fine particles of the reddish dust in the air. In that case, isn't it possible that the dust obscures the night sky so that you don't see anything? Good Lord, it happens often enough in New York City."

Halsted said, "As a matter of fact, the problem in New York isn't so much the dust as the scattered light from the buildings and highways; and even in New York you can see the bright stars, if the sky isn't cloudy.

"On Mars, it would have to work both ways. If there is enough dust to make the sky invisible from the ground, then the ground would be invisible from the sky. For instance, when Mariner 9 reached Mars in 1969, Mars was having a globe-wide duststorm and none of its surface could be seen by Mariner. At that time, from the Martian surface, the sky would have had to be blanked out. Most of the time, though, we see the surface clearly from our probes, so from the Martian surface, the sky would be clearly visible.

"In fact, considering that Mars's atmosphere is much thinner than Earth's—less than a hundredth as thick—it would scatter and absorb far less light than Earth's does, and the various stars and planets would all look a little brighter than they would with Earth's atmosphere in the way. I didn't allow for that in my table."

Trumbull said, "Jeff mentioned the Viking photographs. They show rocks all over the place. Do the

Tri-Luciferians mention rocks?"

"No," said Thatcher, "not that I ever noticed. But again, they don't say there aren't any. They talk about huge canyons and dry river beds and terraced ice-fields."

Rubin snorted. "All that's been known since 1969. More homework."

Avalon said, "What about life? We still don't know if there's any life on Mars. The Viking results are ambiguous. Have the Tri-Luciferians committed themselves on that?"

"Thatcher thought, then said, "I wish I could say I had read all their literature thoroughly, but I haven't. Still, Carol has forced me to read quite a bit since she said I ought not defame anything without learning about it first."

"That's true enough," said Avalon, "though life is short and there are some things that are so unlikely on the surface that one hesitates to devote much of one's time to a study of them. However, can you say anything as to the Tri-Luciferians' attitude toward Martian life from what you've read of their literature?"

Thatcher said, "They speak about Mars's barren surface, its desert aridity and emptiness. They contrast that with the excitement and fullness of the astral sphere."

"Yes," said Avalon, "and of course, the surface *is* dry and empty and barren. We know that much. What about microscopic life? That's what we're looking for."

Thatcher shook his head. "No mention of it, as far as I know."

Avalon said, "Well, then, I can't think of anything else. I'm quite certain this whole thing is nonsense. Everyone here is, and none of us need proof of it. If your wife needs proof, we may not be able to supply it."

"I understand," said Thatcher. "I thank you all, of course, and I suppose she may come to her senses after a while, but I must admit I have never seen her quite like this. I would join the cult with her just to keep her in sight; but, frankly, I'm afraid I'll end up believing it, too."

And in the silence that followed, Henry said softly, "Perhaps Mr. Thatcher, you need not go to that extreme."

Thatcher turned suddenly. "Pardon me. Did you say something, waiter?"

Halsted said, "Henry is a member of the club, Jonathan. I don't know that he's an astronomer exactly, but he's the brightest person here. Is there something we've missed, Henry?"

Henry said, "I think so, sir. You said, Mr. Halsted, that astronomy books don't generally describe any sky but Earth's, and I guess that must be why the cult-leader seems to have a missing item in his description of Mars. Without it, the whole thing is no more true to life than Mr. Rubin's conspiracy of locksmiths—if I may be forgiven, Mr. Rubin."

"Not if you don't supply a missing object. Henry?"

Henry said, "On Earth, Mercury and Venus are the morning and evening stars, and we always think of such objects as planets, therefore. Consequently, from Mars, there must be three morning and evening stars, Mercury, Venus, plus Earth in addition. That is memorialized in the very name of the cult, and from that alone I could see the whole thing fails."

Halsted said, "I'm not sure I see your point, Henry."

"But, Mr. Halsted," said Henry, "where is the Moon in all this? It is a large object, our Moon, almost the size of Mercury and closer to Mars than Mercury is. If Mercury can be seen from Mars, surely the Moon can be, too. Yet I noticed it was not on your list of bright objects in the Martian sky."

Halsted turned red. "Yes, of course. The list of planets fooled me, too. You just list them without mentioning the Moon." He reached for the paper. "The Moon is smaller than Earth and less reflective, so that it is only 1/70 as bright as the Earth, at equal distance and phase which means—a magnitude of 0.0. It would be just as bright as Mercury, and in fact it could be seen more easily than Mercury could be because it would be higher in the sky. At sunset, Mercury as evening star would never be higher than 16 degrees above the horizon, while Earth could be as much as 44 degrees above—pretty high in the sky."

Henry said, "Mars, therefore, would have four morning stars, and the very name, Tri-Lucifer, is nonsense."

Avalon said, "But the Moon would always be close to Earth, so wouldn't Earth's light drown it out?"

"No," said Halsted. "Let's see now. —Never get a pocket computer that doesn't have keys for the trigonometric functions.— The Moon would be, at times, as much as 23 minutes of arc away from Earth, when viewed from Mars. That's three-quarters the width of the Moon as seen from Earth."

Henry said, "One more thing. Would you repeat that verse once again, Mr. Thatcher, the one about the Earth being high in the sky."

Thatcher said, "Certainly. 'When Earth shines high in the sky, like a glorious jewel, and when the other Lucifers have fled beyond the horizon, so that Earth shines alone in splendor, single in beauty, unmatched in brightness, it is then that the souls of those ready to receive the call, must prepare to rise from Earth and cross the gulf.' "

Henry said, "Earth may be quite high in the sky at times, and Mercury and Venus may be on the other side of the Sun and therefore beyond the horizon— but Earth cannot be 'alone in splendor.' The Moon has to be with it. Of course, there would be times when the moon is very nearly in front of Earth or behind it, as seen from Mars, so that the two dots of light merge into one that seems to make Earth brighter than ever, but the Moon is not then beyond the horizon. It seems to me, Mr. Thatcher, that the cult-leader was never on Mars, because if he had been he would not missed a pretty big item, a world 2160 miles across. Surely you can explain this to your wife."

"Yes," said Thatcher, his face brightening into a smile, "She would have to see the whole thing is fake."

"If it is true, as you say," said Henry quietly, "that she is a rational person."

A SOLUTION TO MACHISMO ON BYRONIA
(from page 43)

The Supreme Ruler's plan will not work.

Consider all first-born children. One-third will be male, one-third female, one-third bisexual. Mothers who give birth to bisexuals will be sterilized.

The remaining mothers may have second children. One-third of the second-born will be male, one-third female, one-third bisexual. Again, mothers of the bisexuals will be made sterile.

The remaining mothers may have third children, and so on. This obviously generalizes to families of any size. The proportions of sexes will always be 1:1:1.

Assume that the decree lasts a thousand years and that all mothers live long enough, and are healthy enough, to keep bearing children until they have a bisexual. What will be the average number of children born to a Byronian mother during the millennial period? See page 156 for this answer.

HOME TEAM ADVANTAGE
by Jack C. Haldeman II

*The author reports that he is now 34; he
lives with his wife, Vol, their two
daughters, two cats, and an alligator
in a weathered cedar cabin full of
tree frogs. Mr. Haldeman further reports
hard times in the swamp these days: the
alligators have been seen selling
apples and pencils along the canal.*

Slugger walked down the deserted hallway, his
footsteps making a hollow ringing sound under the
empty stadium. Turning a corner, he headed for the
dugout. He was early. He was always early.
Sportscasters said he'd probably be early for his own
funeral.

He was.

Slugger sat on the wooden bench. It was too quiet.
He picked up a practice bat and tapped it against the
concrete floor. Normally he and Lefty would be raz-
zing Pedro. Coach Weinraub would be pacing up and
down, cursing the players, the umpire. There would
be a lot of noise, gum popping, tobacco spitting, and
good-natured practical jokes. The Kid would be sitting at the far end of the bench, worrying about his
batting average and keeping his place in the starting
lineup. The Kid always did that, even though he had

a .359 average. The Kid was a worrier, but he wouldn't worry anymore. Not after yesterday. Not after the Arcturians won the series and ended the season. Not after they won the right to eat all the humans.

Tough luck about being eaten, but Slugger couldn't let himself feel too bad about that; he had led the league in homers and the team had finished the regular season 15 games out in front. Except for the series with the Arcturians, it had been a good year. Slugger hefted the practice bat over his shoulder and climbed the dugout steps, as he had done so many times before, up to the field. This time there were no cheers.

The early morning wind blew yesterday's hot dog wrappers and beer cups across the infield. It was cool; dew covered the artificial grass, fog drifted in the bleachers. Slugger strode firmly up to the plate, took his stance, and swung hard at an imaginary ball. In his mind there was a solid crack, a roar from the crowd and the phantom ball sailed over the center field fence. He dropped the bat and started to run the bases. By the time he rounded third, he had slowed to a walk. The empty stadium closed in on him, and when he reached home plate he sat down in the batter's box to wait for the Arcturians.

He wasn't alone very long. A television crew drove up in a large van and started setting up their cameras. Some carpenters quickly erected a temporary stage on the pitcher's mound. The ground crew half-heartedly picked up the hot dog wrappers and paper cups. Slugger started back to the dugout but he didn't make it. He ran into the Hawk.

Julius Hawkline was a character, an institution of sorts in the sports world. In his early days as a manager, the Hawk had been crankier and more controversial than the legendary Stengel. In his present role as television announcer and retired S.O.B., the Hawk was more irritating and opinionated than the legendary Cosell. True to his name, the Hawk was descending on Slugger for an interview.

"Hey Slugger!"

"Gotta go."

"Just take a minute." A man was running around with a camera, getting it all on tape. "You owe it to the fans."

The fans. That got to Slugger. It always did.

"Okay, Hawk. Just a minute. Gotta get back to the locker room. The guys'll be there soon."

"How's it feel to have blown the game, the series—to be responsible for the Arcturians earning the right to eat all the humans?"

"We played good," said Slugger, backing away. "They just played better. That's all."

"That's *all?* They're going to *eat* us and you blew it four to three. Not to mention Lefty—"

"Don't blame Lefty. He couldn't help it. Got a trick ankle, that's all."

"*All?* They're going to gobble us up—you know, knives, forks, pepper, Worcestershire sauce, all that stuff; every man, woman, and child. Imagine all those poor children out there covered with catsup. All because of a trick ankle and a couple of bonehead plays. Sure we can blame Lefty. The whole world will blame Lefty, blame you, blame the entire team. You let us down. It's all over, buddy, and your team couldn't win the big one. What do you have to say to that?"

"We played good. They played better."

The Hawk turned from Slugger and faced the camera. "And now you have it, ladies and gentlemen, the latest word from down here on the field while we await the arrival of the Arcturians for their postgame picnic. Slugger says we played good, but let me tell you that this time 'good' just wasn't good enough. We had to be *great* and we just couldn't get it up for the final game. The world will little note nor long remember that Slugger went ten for seventeen in the series, or that we lost the big one by only one run. What they *will* remember is Lefty falling down rounding first, *tripping* over his own shoelaces, causing us to lose the whole ball of wax."

Slugger walked over to the Hawk, teeth clenched. He reached out and crumpled the microphone with one hand.

"Lefty's my friend. We played good." He turned and walked back to the dugout.

The Hawk was delighted. They'd gotten it all on tape.

When Slugger got back to the dressing room, most of the team was there, suiting up. Everything was pretty quiet, there was none of the horseplay that usually preceded a game. Slugger went to his locker and started to dress. Someone had tied his shoelaces together. He grinned. It was a tough knot.

Usually coach Weinraub would analyze the previous day's game—giving pointers, advice, encouragement and cussing a few of the players out. Today he just sat on the bench, eyes downcast. Slugger had to keep reminding himself that there wouldn't be any more games; not today, not tomorrow. Never again. It just didn't seem possible. He slipped his glove on, the worn leather fitting his hand perfectly. It felt good to be in uniform, even if it was just for a picnic.

The noise of the crowd filtered through to the dressing room; the stadium was filling up. The Arcturians would be here soon. Reporters were crowding at the door, slipping inside. Flashbulbs were popping.

Lefty snuck in the back way and slipped over to his locker. It was next to Slugger's. They had been friends a long time, played in the minors together.

"Mornin' Lefty," said Slugger. "How's the wife and kids?"

"Fine," mumbled Lefty, pulling off the false mustache he'd worn to get through the crowd.

"Ankle still bothering you?"

"Naw. It's fine now."

"Can't keep a good man down," said Slugger, patting Lefty on the back.

A microphone appeared between them, followed by

the all too familiar face of the Hawk.

"Hey Lefty, how about a few words for the viewing public? How does it feel to be the meathead that blew the whole thing?"

"Aw, come on, Hawk, gimme a break."

"It was a team effort all the way," said Slugger, reaching for the microphone.

"These things cost money," said the Hawk, stepping back. The coach blew his whistle.

"Come on team, this is it. Everybody topside." The dressing room emptied quickly. Nobody wanted to be around the Hawk. Even being the main course at the picnic was better than that.

On the field the Arcturians had already been introduced and they stood at attention along the third base line. One by one the humans' names were called, and they took their places along the first base line. The crowd cheered Slugger and booed Lefty. Slugger felt bad about that. The stage on the pitcher's mound had a picnic table on it and the Arcturian managers and coaches were sitting around it, wearing bibs.

After they played both planets' anthems, George Alex, the league president, went to the podium set up on the stage.

"Ladies and gentlemen, I won't keep you in suspense much longer. The name of the first human to be eaten will be announced shortly. But first I would like to thank you, the fans, for casting so many ballots to choose the person we will honor today. As with the All-Star game, the more votes that are cast make for a more representative selection. All over the country—the world, for that matter—fans like you, just plain people, have been writing names on the backs of hot dog wrappers and stuffing them in the special boxes placed in all major league stadiums. I'm proud to say that over ten million votes were cast and we have a winner. The envelope, please."

A man in a tuxedo, flanked by two armed guards, presented the envelope.

"The results are clear. The first human to be eaten will be ... the Hawk! Let's hear it for *Julius W. Hawkline!*"

The stadium rocked with cheers. The Hawk was obviously the crowd's favorite. He was, however, reluctant to come forward and had to be dragged to the stage. The other reporters stuck microphones in his face, asking him how it felt to be the chosen one.

For the first time in his life the Hawk was at a loss for words.

The coach of the Arcturians held the Hawk with four of his six arms and ceremoniously bit off his nose. Everyone cheered and the Arcturian chewed. And chewed. The crowd went wild. He chewed some more. Finally, he spat the Hawk's nose out and went into a huddle with the other coaches.

Undigestible was the conclusion, unchewable; humans were definitely inedible. Something else would have to be arranged.

Slugger smiled to himself, thinking ahead to next season. You had to hand it to the Hawk; he was one tough old bird.

AIR RAID
by Herb Boehm

Raised in Texas, Herb Boehm now lives among the tall trees of Oregon—a state that has recently been building up a very respectable population of SF writers. Mr. Boehm tells us he has no occupation but writing; and says that if things keep going as well as they have, he may never have to do another lick of work. He's very much a supporter of the women's movement, trying to people his stories with a majority of females.

I was jerked awake by the silent alarm vibrating my skull. It won't shut down until you sit up, so I did. All around me in the darkened bunkroom the Snatch Team members were sleeping, singly and in pairs. I yawned, scratched my ribs, and patted Gene's hairy flank. He turned over. So much for a romantic send-off.

Rubbing sleep from my eyes, I reached to the floor for my leg, strapped it on and plugged it in. Then I was running down the rows of bunks toward Ops.

The situation board glowed in the gloom. Sun-Belt Airlines Flight 128, Miami to New York, September 15, 1979. We'd been looking for that one for three years. I should have been happy, but who can afford it when you wake up?

Liza Boston muttered past me on the way to Prep. I muttered back, and followed. The lights came on

139

around the mirrors, and I groped my way to one of them. Behind us, three more people staggered in. I sat down, plugged in, and at last I could lean back and close my eyes.

They didn't stay closed for long. Rush! I sat up straight as the sludge I use for blood was replaced with supercharged go-juice. I looked around me and got a series of idiot grins. There was Liza, and Pinky and Dave. Against the far wall Cristabel was already turning slowly in front of the airbrush, getting a caucasian paint job. It looked like a good team.

I opened the drawer and started preliminary work on my face. It is a lot bigger job every time. Transfusion or no, I looked like death. The right ear was completely gone now. I could no longer close my lips; the gums were permanently bared. A week earlier, a finger had fallen off in my sleep. And what's it to you, bugger?

While I worked, one of the screens around the mirror glowed. A smiling young woman, blonde, high brow, round face. Close enough. The crawl line read *Mary Katrina Sondergard, born Trenton, New Jersey, age in 1979: 25*. Baby, this is your lucky day.

The computer melted the skin away from her face to show me the bone structure, rotated it, gave me cross-sections. I studied the similarities with my own skull, noted the differences. Not bad, and better than some I'd been given.

I assembled a set of dentures that included the slight gap in the upper incisors. Putty filled out my cheeks. Contact lenses fell from the dispenser and I popped them in. Nose plugs widened my nostrils. No need for ears; they'd be covered by the wig. I pulled a blank plastiflesh mask over my face and had to pause while it melted in. It took only a minute to mold it to perfection. I smiled at myself. How nice to have lips.

The delivery slot clunked and dropped a blonde wig and a pink outfit into my lap. The wig was hot from the styler. I put it on, then the pantyhose.

"Mandy? Did you get the profile on Sondergard?" I

didn't look up: I recognized the voice.

"Roger."

"We've located her near the airport. We can slip you in before take-off, so you'll be the joker."

I groaned, and looked up at the face on the screen. Elfreda Baltimore-Louisville, Director of Operational Teams: lifeless face and tiny slits for eyes. What can you do when all the muscles are dead?

"Okay." You take what you get.

She switched off, and I spent the next two minutes trying to get dressed while keeping my eyes on the screens. I memorized names and faces of crew members plus the few facts known about them. Then I hurried out and caught up with the others. Elapsed time from first alarm: twelve minutes and seven seconds. We'd better get moving.

"Goddam Sun-Belt," Cristabel groused, hitching at her bra.

"At least they got rid of the high heels," Dave pointed out. A year earlier we would have been teetering down the aisles on three-inch platforms. We all wore short pink shifts with blue and white stripes diagonally across the front, and carried matching shoulder bags. I fussed trying to get the ridiculous pillbox cap pinned on.

We jogged into the dark Operations Control Room and lined up at the gate. Things were out of our hands now. Until the gate was ready, we could only wait.

I was first, a few feet away from the portal. I turned away from it; it gives me vertigo. I focused instead on the gnomes sitting at their consoles, bathed in yellow lights from their screens. None of them looked back at me. They don't like us much. I don't like them, either. Withered, emaciated, all of them. Our fat legs and butts and breasts are a reproach to them, a reminder that Snatchers eat five times their ration to stay presentable for the masquerade. Meantime we continue to rot. One day I'll be sitting at a console. One day I'll be *built in* to a console, with all my guts on the outside and nothing left of my body but stink. The hell with them.

I buried my gun under a clutter of tissues and lipsticks in my purse. Elfreda was looking at me.

"Where is she?" I asked.

"Motel room. She was alone from 10 PM to noon on flight day."

Departure time was 1:15. She cut it close and would be in a hurry. Good.

"Can you catch her in the bathroom? Best of all, in the tub?"

"We're working on it." She sketched a smile with a fingertip drawn over lifeless lips. She knew how I like to operate, but she was telling me I'd take what I got. It never hurts to ask. People are at their most defenseless stretched out and up to their necks in water.

"Go!" Elfreda shouted. I stepped through, and things started to go wrong.

I was faced the wrong way, stepping *out* of the bathroom door and facing the bedroom. I turned and spotted Mary Katrina Sondergard through the haze of the gate. There was no way I could reach her without stepping back through. I couldn't even shoot without hitting someone on the other side.

Sondergard was at the mirror, the worst possible place. Few people recognize themselves quickly, but she'd been looking right at herself. She saw me and her eyes widened. I stepped to the side, out of her sight.

"What the hell is . . . hey? Who the hell . . ." I noted the voice, which can be the trickiest thing to get right.

I figured she'd be more curious than afraid. My guess was right. She came out of the bathroom, passing through the gate as if it wasn't there, which it wasn't, since it only has one side. She had a towel wrapped around her.

"Jesus Christ! What are you doing in my—" Words fail you at a time like that. She knew she ought to

142

say something, but what? *Excuse me, haven't I seen you in the mirror?*

I put on my best stew smile and held out my hand.

"Pardon the intrusion. I can explain everything. You see, I'm—" I hit her on the side of the head and she staggered and went down hard. Her towel fell to the floor. "—working my way through college." She started to get up, so I caught her under the chin with my artificial knee. She stayed down.

"Standard fuggin' *oil*!" I hissed, rubbing my injured knuckles. But there was no time. I knelt beside her, checked her pulse. She'd be okay, but I think I loosened some front teeth. I paused a moment. Lord, to look like that with no make-up, no prosthetics! She nearly broke my heart.

I grabbed her under the knees and wrestled her to the gate. She was a sack of limp noodles. Somebody reached through, grabbed her feet, and pulled. *So long, love! How would you like to go on a long voyage?*

I sat on her rented bed to get my breath. There were car keys and cigarettes in her purse, genuine tobacco, worth its weight in blood. I lit six of them, figuring I had five minutes of my very own. The room filled with sweet smoke. They don't make 'em like that anymore.

The Hertz sedan was in the motel parking lot. I got in and headed for the airport. I breathed deeply of the air, rich in hydrocarbons. I could see for hundreds of yards into the distance. The perspective nearly made me dizzy, but I live for those moments. There's no way to explain what it's like in the pre-meck world. The sun was a fierce yellow ball through the haze.

The other stews were boarding. Some of them knew Sondergard so I didn't say much, pleading a hangover. That went over well, with a lot of knowing laughs and sly remarks. Evidently it wasn't out of character. We boarded the 707 and got ready for the goats to arrive.

It looked good. The four commandos on the other side were identical twins for the women I was working with. There was nothing to do but a stewardess until departure time. I hoped there would be no more glitches. Inverting a gate for a joker run into motel room was one thing, but in a 707 at twenty thousand feet . . .

The plane was nearly full when the woman that Pinky would impersonate sealed the forward door. We taxied to the end of the runway, then we were airborne. I started taking orders for drinks in first.

The goats were the usual lot, for 1979. Fat and sassy, all of them, and as unaware of living in a paradise as a fish is of the sea *What would you think, ladies and gents, of a trip to the future? No? I can't say I'm surprised. What if I told you this plane is going to—*

My alarm beeped as we reached cruising altitude. I consulted the indicator under my Lady Bulova and glanced at one of the restroom doors. I felt a vibration pass through the plane. *Damn it, not so soon.*

The gate was in there, I came out quickly, and motioned for Diana Gleason—Dave's pigeon—to come to the front.

"Take a look at this," I said, with a disgusted look. She started to enter the restroom, stopped when she saw the green glow. I planted a boot on her fanny and shoved. Perfect. Dave would have a chance to hear her voice before popping in. Though she'd be doing little but screaming when she got a look around . . .

Dave came through the gate, adjusting his silly little hat. Diana must have struggled.

"Be disgusted," I whispered.

"What a mess," he said as he came out of the restroom. It was a fair imititation of Diana's tone, though he'd missed the accent. It wouldn't matter much longer.

"What is it?" It was one of the stews from tourist.

We stepped aside so she could get a look, and Dave shoved her through. Pinky popped out very quickly.

"We're minus on minutes," Pinky said. "We lost five on the other side."

"Five?" Dave-Diana squeaked. I felt the same way. We had a hundred and three passengers to process.

"Yeah. They lost contact after you pushed my pigeon through. It took that long to re-align."

You get used to that. Time runs at different rates on each side of the gate, though it's always sequential, past to future. Once we'd started the snatch with me entering Sondergard's room, there was no way to go back any earlier on either side. Here, in 1979, we had a rigid ninety-four minutes to get everything done. On the other side, the gate could never be maintained longer than three hours.

"When you left, how long was it since the alarm went in?"

"Twenty-eight minutes."

It didn't sound good. It would take at least two hours just customizing the wimps. Assuming there was no more slippage on 79-time, we might just make it. But there's *always* slippage. I shuddered, thinking about riding it in.

"No time for any more games, then," I said. "Pink, you go back to tourist and call both of the other girls up here. Tell 'em to come one at a time, and tell 'em we've got a problem. You know the bit."

"Biting back the tears. Got you." She hurried aft. In no time the first one showed up. Her friendly Sun-Belt Airlines smile was stamped on her face, but her stomach would be churning. *Oh God, this is it!*

I took her by the elbow and pulled her behind the curtains in front. She was breathing hard.

"Welcome to the twilight zone," I said, and put the gun to her head. She slumped, and I caught her. Pinky and Dave helped me shove her through the gate.

"Fug! The rotting thing's flickering."

Pinky was right. A very ominous sign. But the

green glow stabilized as we watched, with who-knows-how-much slippage on the other side. Cristabel ducked through.

"We're plus thirty-three," she said. There was no sense talking about what we were all thinking: things were going badly.

"Back to tourist," I said. "Be brave, smile at everyone, but make it just a little bit too good, got it?"

"Check," Cristabel said.

We processed the other quickly, with no incident. Then there was no time to talk about anything. In eighty-nine minutes Flight 128 was going to be spread all over a mountain whether we were finished or not.

Dave went into the cockpit to keep the flight crew out of our hair. Me and Pinky were supposed to take care of first class, then back up Cristabel and Liza in tourist. We used the standard "coffee, tea, or milk" gambit, relying on our speed and their inertia.

I leaned over the first two seats on the left.

"Are you enjoying your flight?" Pop, pop. Two squeezes on the trigger, close to the heads and out of sight of the rest of the goats.

"Hi, folks. I'm Mandy. Fly me." Pop, pop.

Half-way to the galley, a few people were watching us curiously. But people don't make a fuss until they have a lot more to go on. One goat in the back row stood up, and I let him have it. By now there were only eight left awake. I abandoned the smile and squeezed off four quick shots. Pinky took care of the rest. We hurried through curtains, just in time.

There was an uproar building in the back of tourist, with about sixty percent of the goats already processed. Cristabel glanced at me, and I nodded.

"Okay, folks," she bawled. "I want you to be quiet. Calm down and listen up, *You,* fathead, *pipe down* before I cram my foot up your ass sideways."

The shock of hearing her talk like that was enough to buy us a little time, anyway. We had formed a skirmish line across the width of the plane, guns out, steadied on seat backs, aimed at the milling, befuddled group of thirty goats.

The guns are enough to awe all but the most foolhardy. In essence, a standard-issue stunner is just a plastic rod with two grids about six inches apart. There's not enough metal in it to set off a hijack alarm. And to people from the Stone Age to about 2190 it doesn't look any more like a weapon than a ball-point pen. So Equipment Section jazzes them up in a plastic shell to real Buck Rogers blasters, with a dozen knobs and lights that flash and a barrel like the snout of a hog. Hardly anyone ever walks into one.

"We are in great danger, and time is short. You must all do exactly as I tell you, and you will be safe."

You can't give them time to think, you have to rely on your status as the Voice of Authority. The situation is just *not* going to make sense to them, no matter how you explain it.

"Just a minute, I think you owe us—"

An airborne lawyer. I made a snap decision, thumbed the fireworks switch on my gun, and shot him.

The gun made a sound like a flying saucer with hermorrhoids, spit sparks and little jets of flame, and extended a green laser finger to his forehead. He dropped.

All pure kark, of course. But it sure is impressive.

And it's damn risky, too. I had to choose between a panic if the fathead got them to thinking, and a possible panic from the flash of the gun. But when a 20th gets to talking about his "rights" and what he is "owed," things can get out of hand. It's infectious.

It worked. There was a lot of shouting, people ducking behind seats, but no rush. We could have handled it, but we needed some of them conscious if we were ever going to finish the Snatch.

"Get up. Get *up,* you *slugs!*" Cristabel yelled. "He's stunned, nothing worse. But I'll *kill* the next one who gets out of line. Now *get to your feet* and do what I tell you. *Children first! Hurry,* as fast as you can, to the front of the plane. Do what the stewardess tells you. Come on, kids, *move!"*

I ran back into first class just ahead of the kids, turned at the open restroom door, and got on my knees.

They were petrified. There were five of them—crying, some of them, which always chokes me up—looking left and right at dead people in the first class seats, stumbling, near panic.

"Come on, kids," I called to them, giving my special smile. "Your parents will be along in just a minute. Everything's going to be all right, I promise you. Come on."

I got three of them through. The fourth balked. She was determined not to go through that door. She spread her legs and arms and I couldn't push her through. I will *not* hit a child, never. She raked her nails over my face. My wig came off, and she gaped at my bare head. I shoved her through.

Number five was sitting in the aisle, bawling. He was maybe seven. I ran back and picked him up, hugged him and kissed him, and tossed him through. God, I needed a rest, but I was needed in tourist.

"You, you, you, and you. Okay, you too. Help him, will you?" Pinky had a practiced eye for the ones that wouldn't be any use to anyone, even themselves. We herded them toward the front of the plane, then deployed ourselves along the left side where we could cover the workers. It didn't take long to prod them into action. We had them dragging the limp bodies forward as fast as they could go. Me and Cristabel were in tourist, with the others up front.

Adrenalin was being catabolized in my body now; the rush of action left me and I started to feel very tired. There's an unavoidable feeling of sympathy for the poor dumb goats that starts to get me about this stage of the game. Sure, they were better off, sure they were going to die if we didn't get them off the plane. But when they saw the other side they were going to have a hard time believing it.

The first ones were returning for a second load, stunned at what they'd just seen: dozens of people being put into a cubicle that was crowded when it was empty. One college student looked like he'd been hit in the stomach. He stopped by me and his eyes pleaded.

"Look, I want to *help* you people, just . . . what's going *on*? Is this some new kind of rescue? I mean, are we going to crash—"

I switched my gun to prod and brushed it across his cheek. He gasped, and fell back.

"Shut your fuggin' mouth and get moving, or I'll kill you." It would be hours before his jaw was in shape to ask any more stupid questions.

We cleared tourist and moved up. A couple of the work gang were pretty damn pooped by then. Muscles like horses, all of them, but they can hardly run up a flight of stairs. We let some of them go through, including a couple that were at least fifty years old. *Je*-fuzz. Fifty! We got down to a core of four men and two women who seemed strong, and worked them until they nearly dropped. But we processed everyone in twenty-five minutes.

The portapak came through as we were stripping off our clothes. Cristabel knocked on the door to the cockpit and Dave came out, already naked. A bad sign.

"I had to cork 'em," he said. "Bleeding Captain just *had* to made his Grand March through the plane. I tried *every*thing."

Sometimes you have to do it. The plane was on autopilot, as it normally would be at this time. But if any of us did anything detrimental to the craft, changed the fixed course of events in any way, that would be it. All that work for nothing, and Flight 128 inaccessible to us for all Time. I don't know sludge about time theory, but I know the practical angles. We can do things in the past only at times

149

and in places where it won't make any difference. We have to cover our tracks. There's flexibility; once a Snatcher left her gun behind and it went in with the plane. Nobody found it, or if they did, they didn't have the smoggiest idea of what it was, so we were okay.

Flight 128 was mechanical failure. That's the best kind; it means we don't have to keep the pilot unaware of the situation in the cabin right down to ground level. We can cork him and fly the plane, since there's nothing he could have done to save the flight anyway. A pilot-error smash is almost impossible to Snatch. We mostly work mid-airs, bombs, and structural failures. If there's even one survivor, we can't touch it. It would not fit the fabric of space-time, which is immutable (though it can stretch a little), and we'd all just fade away and appear back in the ready-room.

My head was hurting. I wanted that portapak very badly.

"Who has the most hours on a 707?" Pinky did, so I sent her to the cabin, along with Dave, who could do the pilot's voice for air traffic control. You have to have a believable record in the flight recorder, too. They trailed two long tubes from the portapak, and the rest of us hooked in up close. We stood there, each of us smoking a fistful of cigarettes, wanting to finish them but hoping there wouldn't be time. The gate had vanished as soon as we tossed our clothes and the flight crew through.

But we didn't worry long. There's other nice things about Snatching, but nothing to compare with the rush of plugging into a portapak. The wake-up transfusion is nothing but fresh blood, rich in oxygen and sugars. What we were getting now was an insane brew of concentrated adrenalin, super-saturated hemoglobin, methedrine, white lightning, TNT, and Kickapoo joyjuice. It was like a firecracker in your heart; a boot in the box that rattled your sox.

"I'm growing hair on my chest," Cristabel said,

solemnly. Everyone giggled.

"Would someone hand me my eyeballs?"

"The blue ones, or the red ones?"

"I think my ass just fell off."

We'd heard them all before, but we howled anyway. We were strong, *strong,* and for one golden moment we had no worries. Everything was hilarious. I could have torn sheet metal with my eyelashes.

But you get hyper on that mix. When the gage didn't show, and didn't show, and *didn't sweetjeez show* we all started milling. This bird wasn't going to fly all that much longer.

Then it did show, and we turned on. The first of the wimps came through, dressed in the clothes taken from a passenger it had been picked to resemble.

"Two thirty-five elapsed upside time," Cristabel announced.

"Je-zuz."

It is a deadening routine. You grab the harness around the wimp's shoulders and drag it along the aisle, after consulting the seat number painted on its forehead. The paint would last three minutes. You seat it, strap it in, break open the harness and carry it back to toss through the gate as you grab the next one. You have to take it for granted they've done the work right on the other side: fillings in the teeth, fingerpints, the right match in height and weight and hair color. Most of those things don't matter much, especially on Flight 128 which was a crash-and-burn. There would be bits and pieces, and burned to a crisp at that. But you can't take chances. Those rescue workers are pretty thorough on the parts they *do* find; the dental work and fingerprints especially are important.

I hate wimps. I really hate 'em. Every time I grab the harness of one of them, if it's a child, I wonder if it's Alice. *Are you my kid, you vegetable, you slug, you slimy worm?* I joined the Snatchers right after the brain bugs ate the life out of my baby's head. I couldn't stand to think she was the last generation, that the last humans there would ever be would live with nothing in their heads, medically dead by standards that prevailed even in 1979, with computers working their muscles to keep them in tone. You grow up, reach puberty still fertile—one in a thousand—rush to get pregnant in your first heat. Then you find out your mom or pop passed on a chronic disease bound right into the genes, and none of your kids will be immune. I *knew* about the paraleprosy; I grew up with my toes rotting away. But this was too much. What do you do?

Only one in ten of the wimps had a customized face. It takes time and a lot of skill to build a new face that will stand up to a doctor's autopsy. The rest came pre-mutilated. We've got millions of them; it's not hard to find a good match in the body. Most of them would stay breathing, too dumb to stop, until they went in with the plane.

The plane jerked, hard. I glanced at my watch. Five minutes to impact. We should have time. I was on my last wimp. I could hear Dave frantically calling the ground. A bomb came through the gate, and I tossed it into the cockpit. Pinky turned on the pressure sensor on the bomb and came running out, followed by Dave. Liza was already through. I grabbed the limp dolls in stewardess costume and tossed them to the floor. The engine fell off and a piece of it came through the cabin. We started to depressurize. The bomb blew away part of the cockpit (the ground crash crew would read it—we hoped—that part of the engine came through and killed the crew: no more words from the pilot on the flight recorder) and we turned, slowly, left and down. I was lifted toward the hole in the side of the plane, but I managed to hold onto a seat. Cristabel wasn't so lucky. She was blown backwards.

We started to rise slightly, losing speed. Suddenly it was uphill from where Cristabel was lying in the aisle. Blood oozed from her temple. I glanced back;

everyone was gone, and three pink-suited wimps were piled on the floor. The plane began to stall, to nose down, and my feet left the floor.

"Come on, Bel!" I screamed. That gate was only three feet away from me, but I began pulling myself along to where she floated. The plane bumped, and she hit the floor. Incredibly, it seemed to wake her up. She started to swim toward me, and I grabbed her hand as the floor came up to slam us again. We crawled as the plane went through its final death agony, and we came to the door. The gate was gone.

There wasn't anything to say. We were going in. It's hard enough to keep the gate in place on a plane that's moving in a straight line. When a bird gets to corkscrewing and coming apart, the math is fearsome. So I've been told.

I embraced Cristabel and held her bloodied head. She was groggy, but managed to smile and shrug. You take what you get. I hurried into the restroom and got both of us down on the floor. Back to the forward bulkhead, Cristabel between my legs, back to front. Just like in training. We pressed our feet against the other wall. I hugged her tightly and cried on her shoulder.

And it was there. A green glow to my left. I threw myself toward it, dragging Cristabel, keeping low as two wimps were thrown head-first through the gate above our heads. Hands grabbed and pulled us through. I clawed my way a good five yards along the floor. You can leave a leg on the other side and I didn't have one to spare.

I sat up as they were carrying Cristabel to Medical. I patted her arm as she went by on the stretcher, but she was passed out. I wouldn't have minded passing out myself.

For a while, you can't believe it all really happened. Sometimes it turns out it *didn't* happen. You come back and find out all the goats in the holding pen have softly and suddenly vanished away because the continuum won't tolerate the changes and paradoxes you've put into it. The people you've worked so hard to rescue are spread like tomato surprise all over some goddam hillside in Carolina and all you've got left is a bunch of ruined wimps and an exhausted Snatch Team. But not this time. I could see the goats milling around in the holding pen, naked and more bewildered than ever. And just starting to be *really* afraid.

Elfreda touched me as I passed her. She nodded, which meant well-done in her limited repertoire of gestures. I shrugged, wondering if I cared, but the surplus adrenalin was still in my veins and I found myself grinning at her. I nodded back.

Gene was standing by the holding pen. I went to him, hugged him. I felt the juices start to flow. *Damn it, let's squander a little ration and have us a good time.*

Someone was beating on the sterile glass wall of the pen. She shouted, mouthing angry words at us. *Why? What have you done to us?* It was Mary Sondergard. She implored her bald, one-legged twin to make her understand. She thought she had problems. God, was she pretty. I hated her guts.

Gene pulled me away from the wall. My hands hurt, and I'd broken off all my fake nails without scratching the glass. She was sitting on the floor now, sobbing. I heard the voice of the briefing officer on the outside speaker.

". . . Centauri 3 is hospitable, with an Earth-like climate. By that, I mean *your* Earth, not what it has become. You'll see more of that later. The trip will take five years, shiptime. Upon landfall, you will be entitled to one horse, a plow, three axes, two hundred kilos of seed grain . . ."

I leaned against Gene's shoulder. At their lowest ebb, this very moment, they were so much better than us. I had maybe ten years, half of that as a basketcase. They are our best, our very brightest hope. Everything is up to them.

". . . that no one will be forced to go. We wish to

point out again, not for the last time, that you would all be dead without our intervention. There are things you should know, however. You cannot breathe our air. If you remain on Earth, you can never leave this building. We are not like you. We are the result of a genetic winnowing, a mutation process. We are the survivors, but our enemies have evolved along with us. They are winning. You, however, are immune to the diseases that afflict us . . ."

I winced, and turned away.

". . . the other hand, if you emigrate you will be given a chance at a new life. It won't be easy, but as Americans you should be proud of your pioneer heritage. Your ancestors survived, and so will you. It can be a rewarding experience, and I urge you . . ."

Sure. Gene and I looked at each other and laughed. *Listen to this, folks. Five percent of you will suffer nervous breakdowns in the next few days, and never leave. About the same number will commit suicide, here and on the way. When you get there, sixty to seventy percent will die in the first three years. You will die in childbirth, be eaten by animals, bury two out of three of your babies, starve slowly when the rains don't come. If you live, it will be to break your back behind a plow, sun-up to dusk. New Earth is Heaven, folks!*

God, how I wish I could go with them.

A SECOND SOLUTION TO MACHISMO ON BYRONIA
(from page 132)

Let n be the number of mothers during the thousand-year period.

$n \times 1 = n$ children will be first-born,

$n \times \frac{2}{3} = 2n/3$ children will be second-born,

$n \times \frac{2}{3} \times \frac{2}{3} = 4n/9$ children will be third-born,

$n \times \frac{2}{3} \times \frac{2}{3} \times \frac{2}{3} = 8n/27$ children will be fourth-born, and so on.

The total number of children will be:

$$n + 2n/3 + 4n/9 + 8n/27 + \ldots$$

The limit of this sum is $3n$. There are n mothers, therefore the average number of children per mother is $3n/n = 3$.

There is no need, however, to get involved with an infinite sequence that converges. Can you think of a simple solution that avoids algebra altogether? See page 223 for the answer.

A SIMPLE OUTSIDE JOB
by Robert Lee Hawkins

The author tells us that he was born 23 years ago and raised on a small farm in Ohio. He is, he says, of that unique breed, American-hillbilly/Japanese (the latter on his mother's side of the family). He has a B.S. in physics from Ohio State and is now studying upper-atmosphere physics at Denver University. Hobbies include basketball and football, computers, and the philosophy of science. Mr. Hawkins reports that our purchase of this story—his first sale—was especially cheering since it reached him in the middle of final exams week.

Jeffrey Castilho used the mirrors in one corner of the airlock to check the back of his lifepack, his eyes going from the checklist painted on the wall to the fasteners and connectors of his suit, speaking each item out loud just as he'd been trained. Static muttered in his earphones, from the fusion generator equipment working outside on Titan's surface and inside Titan Pilot Project's lifedome. Then the earphones popped and Jeff heard, "Castilho, this is Rogers. You sure you don't want someone to come with you?"

Jeff tried to scowl and tongue the transmit button at the same time. He caught sight of his face in the mirror, with the stringy beard he'd started to grow when he'd found that no one outside of translunar space shaved, and realized he just looked funny. He took a breath to be sure he kept the irritation out of his voice and said, "No. It's just a matter of plugging in a new black box, and I know you have other things to do."

"Okay. You need help, just holler."

"Sure. Thanks." Jeff tongued the button off and said to the dead microphone, "You don't have to baby me."

Then he looked over the front of his suit: the replacement box for the broken icecube maker, test socket and adaptor, flashlight, screwdrivers, emergency oxygen tank. He'd be damned if he'd take a chance on leaving something behind and asking Rogers to bring it out. He planned on being an asset to Titan Pilot Project, not a liability.

Jeff punched the cycle button and felt his pressure suit become full as the airlock was evacuated. Anyway, he thought, I might be fresh out of engineering school, first time past the orbit of Luna, and earth-grown, but anyone short of a Self-Fulfillment Class dropout could handle this job. No matter what the Shift Supervisor thinks.

The outer door opened and Jeff stepped onto the orange-yellow surface of Titan. He felt the cold—not with his skin, but with his eyes: the dim light of the sun casting unnaturally sharp shadows, the fanciful shapes of melted and refrozen ice, orange-yellow snow drifted by the thin methane wind. Jeff looked closer. It wasn't snow, but chips of eroded ice.

Irritation fell away. This was his dream. Space-living man was self-sufficient in metals, oxygen, and silicon, but short of carbon, nitrogen, and hydrogen—especially hydrogen to be thrown away in his inefficient fusion drives. Titan had all three, carbon in the atmosphere as methane, nitrogen frozen in the ground as ammonia, hydrogen in everything. If Titan Pilot Project proved the feasibility of using these resources, dependence on earth for organic chemicals would end. Jeffrey Castilho was proud to be part of the Project, even if it only meant fixing broken icecube makers.

He found the broken machine a few hundred meters from the lifedome. It was an irregular, dull-silver box, the size of the front half of a railroad boxcar. It had cut a geometrically perfect trench, just wide enough for its caterpillar treads and one-and-a-half meters deep. A double row of transparent water-ice cubes, as tall as Jeff, lay in the trench behind it.

Jeff carefully pushed in the safeties at the snout end of the machine, making sure the lasers wouldn't cut back in when he replaced the bad circuit. The lasers, radiating at a wavelength in the infrared strongly absorbed by water but not by methane, were supposed to melt the orange-yellow ice just ahead of the snout. The machine would then suck in the water, separate the dissolved ammonia and organic contaminants, let a cube start to freeze and drop it out the back. The cubes were shells of ice twenty or thirty centimeters thick filled with liquid water, but quickly froze solid. Plastic balloons of frozen ammonia were dropped off to one side.

But a monitor circuit in the laser control box had gone bad ten minutes before. The icecube maker's brain had turned the lasers off, signaled the main computer, and waited. The job had gone on the job board and Jeff had grabbed it.

Jeff moved to the snout end, shuffling in the low gravity. The lasers were mounted in blisters, connected by a thick wedge that formed an overhang over a pit where the melted water lay. He used his flashlight to find the access hatch, on the lower surface of the wedge.

There was a thin layer of ice covering about fifteen centimeters of liquid in the pit. The ice broke when Jeff dropped into the pit and crawled between the blisters, but he ignored it. His boots were well insulated.

Replacing the module should have been simple enough, but crouched down under the snout, in a pressure suit, trying to work in the crowded circuit compartment by the light of a flash velcroed to one leg, it took a frustratingly long time. Finally Jeff got the black box out and wired into the test socket. Then he plugged the socket into his suit radio and let it talk to the main computer in high-pitched whistles that changed almost too fast to hear. It sounded like a cage full of birds speeded up by a factor of ten. The computer replied vocally:

"Test: module micro 1777496 dash LOC5028: module defective: failure parameters follow. . . ."

Well, he had the right one. Jeff noticed that his helmet was fogging up. The icecube maker's internal heaters were still going, and he was getting vapor—probably ammonia—condensing and freezing on the faceplate. He turned up the faceplate defogger and went back to work, plugging in the new module and checking its operation. Then he hung the old module on his belt, fastened the access hatch shut again, and started to shuffle out from under the snout.

Except his feet wouldn't come.

He swore peevishly and jerked his left foot. The foot shifted inside the boot but the boot didn't move. Jeff twisted to see past his spacesuited legs and swore again.

He had little experience in swearing, but he gave it his best shot. The water in the pit that had been fifteen centimeters deep was now only half that, and there was a thick cylinder of ice around his boots all the way to the ankles.

For a second Jeff felt as cold as if he'd been naked in the methane wind. In the next second his tongue went automatically to the transmit button, but he took it back.

"Wait a minute. I must look like an *idiot*." If he called for help, would Rogers volunteer to come get him? What would the rescue party say when they saw him, crouched between the laser blisters, face in the corner, ankle-deep in dirty ice? "He expected me to screw up. Son-of-a—"

Jeff took three deep breaths. Then he tried chipping with a screwdriver, but the orange-yellow stuff was incredibly tough. He suspected new ice was freezing as fast as he chipped it off. "Couldn't wait for all the water to freeze? Had to jump right in and go wading, eh? Gahhh." Jeff stuck the screwdriver back on his belt. "It might be even stupider not to call for help. Still . . ."

He took his flashlight apart and shorted a wire from the test socket across the battery terminals. The wire glowed a cheery red in the dimness and was almost white-hot when Jeff applied it to the collar of ice around his right ankle. As far as he could tell, it sank right in, losing its glow, but the water seemed to freeze behind it as fast as it melted. Then the wire came loose from one terminal, sparking briefly, and was stuck fast in the ice.

"Great. I should have brought a blowtorch with me." Jeff crouched in the darkness for a while, still not willing to use his radio. And then he started to straighten up with a jerk, thumping his helmet on the overhang, and looked down at his emergency oxygen tank in a wild surmise.

§ § §

The inner airlock door cycled open. With the green emergency tank dangling from his left hand, Jeffrey Castilho stepped into the cloakroom. While he was racking the pressure suit, Rogers stopped in.

"Took you a long time to finish that job, Castilho. No trouble, was there?"

Rogers's face was hard to read behind his thick black beard. Jeff made a vague motion with one hand. "Well, uh—"

Rogers saw the empty emergency tank. "What's that empty for?"

"Well—" Jeff bit the bullet. "I emptied it. I, uh, used it to build a fire."

"A fire."

Jeff's thumb indicated the outside. "People on earth used to burn methane all the time. So I burned some because my feet were stuck in the ice."

"Ah ha. So. You were stupid enough to get stuck." Jeff winced. "But smart enough to get loose." Rogers looked at Jeff for a moment. "I guess we'll settle for that.

"Now, we've been having some trouble with the methane compressors. . . ."

TIME AND HAGAKURE
by Steven Utley

> *Of himself, Mr. Utley reports that his
> is a sedentary life. His interests in-
> clude dinosaurs, the Battle of Little
> Bighorn, and the guitar, which he admits
> he plays rather less brilliantly than,
> say, A. Segovia or J. Beck. Now 28, the
> writer lives in Austin, Texas, one of
> a number of excellent new writers there.*

Inoue stepped into his apartment, closed the door
and found himself on a sparsely wooded hillside. Not
far from where he stood, a shaggy titan scratched its
haunch and belched awesomely. Storm clouds were
gathering in the sky overhead.

Inoue groped his way along the wall until he
bumped into a chair. He eased himself down into it.
From a table beside the chair, he plucked a photograph and held it as though it were a talisman. The
phantom Megatherium went down on all fours and
began tearing at the earth with its long, curved
claws. Ghost lightning flashed on the horizon.

Control, Inoue told himself. He forced himself to
concentrate on the picture, a curling yellow snapshot
of a woman whose face reflected years of strain,
whose eyes had once seen the sun touch the earth.
Opaque eyes; blind, burnt eyes.

Across the room, the enormous ground sloth mooed
softly, then shimmered and dissolved. The Pleis-
tocene thunderheads swirled away.

Inoue studied cracks in the dirty plaster ceiling.
Good, he thought, good. Don't let it run away with
you. You have to be able to control it for a while
closer each time. Relax. Relax.

He settled into the cushions and closed his eyes.
He could feel the power coiled within, tensed to
strike at him if he let it, tensed and ready to do his

163

bidding if he made it.

He took a deep breath, and he began.

§   §   §

The floor disappears as Tadashi starts to swing his legs over the edge of the cot. He stares down through the sky. Far below, silhouetted against a bright sea, the dark gnats of many airplanes swirl about angrily. As he watches, one of the gnats flares up like a match and drops toward the ocean, trailing a fine ribbon of burning gasoline and oily smoke. Tadashi pulls his legs back and huddles upon the cot. A wailing noise fills his ears.

"Lieutenant!"

He starts and looks up from the air battle. At the far edge of the sky, where the horizon merges with the wall of the hut, stands a glowering giant, fists on hips.

"What's the matter with you?" the giant demands. "Can't you hear the sirens?"

Tadashi shakes his head helplessly. His gaze returns to the dogfight. Two more airplanes are going down. The sea ripples, then yields to the familiar wooden planks. The airplanes vanish, swallowed up in the chinks between the planks. Tadashi rubs his eyes.

"Are you all right?" the giant says in a more solicitous tone.

"I . . . Captain Tsuyuki?"

"Of course! Aren't you well, Lieutenant?"

Tadashi puts his feet on the floor and is relieved to feel fine splinters tickling his soles. He rises and sways unsteadily, his head suddenly light, his stomach buoyant. "I'll be all right, sir. I was—the siren! Bombers!"

"They're going for the Yokosuka-Tokyo area," says the captain as Tadashi snatches up his jacket and boots. "The mechanics are warming up the planes. Get into the air immediately!"

Tadashi crams his feet into the boots and clomps past Captain Tsuyuki.

Inoue became aware of the pain mounting behind his eyes and cursed softly as he slipped away from Lieutenant Tadashi Okido. He slumped in his chair, massaging his temples, then got up and went to the window. Outside, the lights of Tokyo held back the night.

When, in the forty-third year of his life, the power had first manifested itself, had begun running amok inside his head, Inoue's Tokyo—dirty, over-crowded, very dangerous Tokyo—started to hold new terrors for him. Thuggee stranglers stalked their victims through the corridors of his apartment complex. Barbarian hordes rode down out of the sky to lay waste to crude towns and villages that lay superimposed upon the dreary confusion of the metropolis. Assyrian, Roman, and Aztec priests wandered past the shrines of the city, and sun-blackened slaves labored to erect pyramids. Waves of mounted knights broke under black rains of arrows from long bows. Volcanoes loomed over the skyline and blew themselves to atoms. Prehistoric glaciers crunched along the highway to Kyoto, and monster-infested coal forests reclaimed boulevards.

Three hundred million years of ghosts filled his head and spilled out into his world.

He returned to his chair and picked up the photograph again and stared into the woman's eyes, the blind, burnt eyes, the eyes seared, ruined, made useless, that time when the sun had come down to engulf Nagasaki.

It had been in the fifth month of his affliction that she came to him the first time. Bent over the lathe, he had glanced up to discover a small garden where the north wall of his tool and die shop was supposed to be. The woman stood there, looking younger than he could recall having ever seen her in life. But he knew her. He had some of the ancient photographs, pictures of her in her bridal attire and drab wartime kimono.

Her gaze was fixed on a point behind and slightly above his head. Awe and terror were creeping into her expression, and a brilliant light made her seem as pale as paraffin. She opened her small mouth and uttered a soundless scream. Her hands rose to her face to claw at her eyes. She fell prone, still screaming, still silent.

Crouched over his lathe, Inoue had reached out for her and caught just a word.

He had seen her several times more in the weeks and months that followed. The scene was always the same; once, though, an enormous iguanodon wandered past, unmindful of the furies raging all around it, unmindful of the stricken woman. Each time, Inoue tried to reach her, to hold tight to her. Each time, he caught only the single word.

Inoue folded his hand over the photograph and forced himself to concentrate and slipped away murmuring the word, the name, *Tadashi, Tadashi* . . .

§ § §

Tadashi is wedging himself into the cockpit of his airplane. Jerking his fur-lined flying helmet down over his close-cropped skull. Waving the ground crew out of the way. Rolling forward, gaining speed. Up. Up. Retract the landing gear. Up. **listen** Up. Three thousand feet and climbing. Young Shiizaki, Tadashi's new wing-man, is a poor pilot whose ship makes known its resentment of his heavy hand. Tadashi grimaces in annoyance and signals Shiizaki to remain in position. Seven thousand feet and climbing. **listen to me** Eight thousand feet. Nine. There is a stab of pain between Tadashi's eyes. **please listen to me** He blinks it away.

§ § §

It had taken Inoue another year to locate the man Tadashi. The stream of Time was a twisting, treacherous one. Inoue cast himself into those waters and discovered what it was to have been a mastodon asphyxiating in a tar pool. He experienced the terror and agony of a Russian officer being torn to pieces by mutinous soldiers. He was a Cro-Magnon woman succumbing to hunger and cold. He bore children. He raped and was raped. He decapitated a man. He was drawn and quartered. He knew moments of peace. He ate strange foods and spoke odd languages. He made love with a filthy Saxon woman and with a rancid Spanish nobleman. He cast himself into the waters of Time again and again, and he felt himself drawn closer to his objective every sixth or seventh attempt, and then, finally, at last—

Tadashi is wedging himself into the cockpit of his airplane. Jerking his fur-lined flying helmet down over his close-cropped skull. Waving the ground crew out of the way. Rolling forward, gaining speed. Up. Up. Away.

§   §   §

Tadashi cruises at seventeen thousand feet, tense behind the controls of the obsolete Zero-Sen fighter. The almost-daily air raids, the seemingly interminable howling of the sirens, the endless mad scrambles to waiting planes, are taking their toll. He had been having difficulty keeping his food down lately, and food is hardly so abundant anymore that it can be wasted in such a manner. His head hurts intermittently. He has been making too many mistakes in the air, overshooting targets, firing his guns too soon or too late and, always, for too long. Ammunition thrown away, wasted in ineffectual feints at the enemy bombers' shiny aluminum bellies.

Gone is the sure, deadly aim, gone the lightning-quick reflexes that made him an ace over the Philippines. He will, he knows, make the final mistake very soon now, and then a Hellcat or a Mustang will blow him out of the air. A precious airplane lost, thrown away in a moment of inattention or confusion.

And what of your wife? Tadashi frowns behind his goggles and reproaches himself. He will only hasten his own end if he permits his mind to wander thus.

He is, he tells himself, a warrior. If he dies, he will

die a warrior's death and ascend to Yasukuni Shrine. He will sell his life dearly, for that is his duty and his honor. *Hagakure,* the Bushido code, is too deeply engrained in him. He cannot imagine alternatives to that code— "A Samurai lives in such a way that he will always be prepared to die" —or to the Emperor's precepts to all soldiers and sailors of Japan: ". . . be resolved that duty is heavier than a mountain, while death is lighter than a feather."

Tadashi catches the flash of sunlight on unpainted aluminum in the distance. He wags his wings to attract Shiizaki's attention and points, then has to bank sharply as Shiizaki, craning his neck to search for the enemy formation, lets his plane swerve toward Tadashi's. Tadashi waves his clumsy wing-man back into position and mentally curses both the lack of radios, which have been removed to lighten the Zero-Sens, and the scarcity of fully trained flyers. He opens the throttle and begins closing the gap between himself and the bombers.

In the space of a year, the Americans' B-29's have flattened virtually the whole of Japanese industry, have severely decimated populations in the major cities, have brought his homeland to its knees. The B-29's are gigantic aircraft, by far the largest he has ever seen. Their size notwithstanding, they are almost as fast as his interceptor, well armed and strong, altogether insuperable machines. Some of them have been brought down, but not many, not enough, and, for the most part, the behemoths seem discouragingly unconcerned with both fighters and flak.

Tadashi feels his guts drawing up into a tight, hard knot as he begins his approach. *Perhaps this is the day,* a part of him whispers, and he clamps his teeth on his lower lip, trying to repress the murmur of panic. The rearmost B-29 in the formation swells in his gunsight. He thumbs off the safety switch, checks his range-finder and opens fire. Tracers simultaneously spit from the bomber's tail guns. There is the whine of a ricochet. Tadashi flinches, scowls, completes his firing pass, kicks the rudder to the left to check on Shiizaki.

Stitched by tracers, Shiizaki's Zéro-Sen sweeps past the B-29, turns on its side and explodes.

you must listen to me think of her the war will soon be over and she will need you in the hard times to follow go back and land and call her to you without delay please please listen to me.

Tadashi grimly drops into position behind a second bomber. But the American plane suddenly shimmers and dances in the sky before him, refusing to stay neatly framed in the gunsight. His eyes throb, his head hurts. The Zero-Sen wobbles sickeningly as his hand slips on the control stick. **I CAN SAVE US ALL IF YOU WILL LISTEN TO ME** and for just a moment he is deaf to the roar and vibration of his plane, removed, face to oddly familiar face with a middle-aged man whose furrowed brow glistens with perspiration, whose eyes are screwed tight with some great effort. Tadashi gives a cry of alarm, and the man appears to gasp and then smiles. The face shatters into scintillae of light. His bride reclines with him in semi-gloom, her skin slick with post-coital perspiration, her delicate fingers tracing patterns on his shoulder and breast as she whispers endearments, *I love you, Tadashi, I shall always love and honor you, stay with me, stay with me, with me, we shall have fine, brave sons and graceful daughters.* He blinks, perplexed, filled with longing, and opens his mouth to speak to her. The soothing liquid flow of her voice is rudely terminated by the sound of canopy glass shattering. A sliver gashes his cheek. He wrenches himself away from his wedding night and finds himself bearing down on the B-29. He cannot remember how to fire his guns.

I don't need to shoot, he thinks. The moisture is gone from his mouth. I don't need to shoot.

break away I've seen you do this many times too many times I am tired sickened by the vio-

lence I've been going mad because of what happened what is going to happen at Nagasaki there is no way to stop the ghosts except by coming to you making you break off this futile engagement Japan is doomed nothing you can do now can change that you can only return to your base and save yourself your wife me

Tadashi shakes his head savagely and gropes for the throttle. Finds it. Opens it to overboost. no no no *no no* NO NO, a scream behind his eyes, the words tumbling out, running together, *nonono,* and the Zero-Sen leaps forward.

§ § §

Inoue moaned, drew himself into a ball, quivered in his chair, sweat popping from every pore, fingers digging into scalp, teeth grinding together.

Then he realized that he had crumpled the photograph. He smoothed it out, whimpering softly to himself. A brittle corner had broken off. He found the wedge-shaped chip of paper in his lap and placed it on the table.

I can do it, he thought, I've made little ripples in Time, I've made him feel my presence, made him see, hear, feel things. I've broken through to him at last, he understands now, he's going to listen this time. I'm going to save us all.

But his headache was worse now. He put the picture into the pocket of his shirt and tiredly rubbed his face for a moment before getting up to go to the window again. He took the picture from his pocket and carefully cupped it in his hand. He regarded the dead eyes sadly.

He had tried, so many times, to reach her and warn her away from the doomed city. Had tried and failed: only that moment of her terror in the garden was open to him.

He had tried to return to the day, early that last month of the war, when Lieutenant Tadashi Okido had sent his young bride to stay with his uncle in Nagasaki. Had tried and failed: only an hour of another, later day in the lieutenant's life was open to him.

He had been trying for weeks to cut short the lieutenant's mission of interception.

He was being driven mad in a Tokyo overrun with phantoms which he alone could see, and Lieutenant Tadashi Okido was his one hope. The Samurai Tadashi, who had to be made, somehow, convinced, somehow, to return to the airfield and call his wife away from Nagasaki.

Tadashi, who, in sending her to that place, had unknowingly cursed Inoue with the power.

This time, Inoue thought, this time it must not happen as it did.

§ § §

LISTEN TO ME YOU MUSTN'T DIE HERE AND NOW YOU MUST LIVE LONG ENOUGH TO SAVE YOUR WIFE AND MY SANITY YOU OWE IT TO US TO LIVE LISTEN ALL THE REMAINING YEARS OF HER LIFE WILL BE A TORMENT WITHOUT YOU AND Tadashi shakes his head savagely and gropes for **MY LIFE HAS BECOME HELL BECAUSE OF YOU** the throttle **YOU AND YOU ALONE** finds it **CAN SAVE US** opens it to **PLEASE LISTEN** opens it to **LISTEN** opens it to overboost, and the Zero-Sen leaps forward to plow through the bomber's tail assembly. The shivering fighter's starboard wing buckles like pasteboard and disintegrates. The cowling shoots away as the radial engine begins disgorging pistons. The Japanese and American planes fall away from each other, fall away spinning, throwing off pieces of themselves.

damn you

§ § §

A large pterodactyl soared past the window. Sobbing with frustration, Inoue pressed his fist against the grimy pane. Go away, Go away. Go away.

He looked at the photograph in his hand, and he said to the woman with the ruined eyes, I found him,

I spoke to him, told him, showed him what was at stake. I invaded the past, I altered it a very little, but why doesn't he listen? Why does he keep doing it? What's wrong with him? Why can't I make him understand?

And he cried out, "Mother, doesn't he even *care?*"

§ § §

Slammed and held by centrifugal force against the wall of the cockpit, Tadashi dazedly listens to his wife's pleas and feels her hands rove down over his body, and he tells her that he loves her, has loved her from the moment he first glimpsed her in her father's house, will love her always, and he tells her that their children, yes, their children will be fine, beautiful children, and he bids her goodbye, knowing she is proud of him now and will follow his example should the need to do so arise, for he is a warrior, with a wife worthy of a warrior, he has abided by the dictates of *Hagakure* and is assured of his place of honor at Yasukuni Shrine, and it is intensely hot and bright in the cockpit, there are screams which may be his own, but he is resolved that duty is heavier than a mountain, while death is li—

COMING OF AGE IN HENSON'S TUBE
by William Jon Watkins

> Bill Watkins is a 34-year-old Associate
> Professor at Brookdale Community College in
> New Jersey, where he teaches the Novel,
> Science Fiction, Creative Writing, and Poetry.
> His fourth novel, written with E. V. Snyder,
> The Litany of Sh'reev, is due from Doubleday
> this month. Mr. Watkins's present hobbies are
> surviving motorcycle crashes and putting his
> bike back together.

Lobber ran in shouting like it was already too late. "Keri's gone Skyfalling! Keri's gone Skyfalling!" He was the kind of kid you naturally ignore, so he had to shout *every*thing. I ignored him. Moody didn't. It made no difference. Lobber went right on shouting. "I saw him going up the Endcap with his wings!"

Moody shouted right back. "Why didn't you stop him?!"

"Who? Me?!! Nobody can stop Keri when he wants to do something. He's crazy!" Lobber was right, of course. Keri *was* crazy; always putting himself in danger for the fun of it, always coming out in one piece. You couldn't stop him. Even Moody couldn't, and Moody was his older brother.

Moody grabbed a pair of Close-ups and started for the door. "He better *not* be Skyfalling! He's too young!"

That almost made me laugh really, because we were *all* too young. But Moody had done it two years ago without getting caught, and I had done it last year. Lobber would never do it. I guess that was why he shouted so much. If you even mentioned it to him, he'd say, "Are you crazy?! You could get killed doing that!"

And he was right about that too. Every couple

173

years, somebody would wait too long to open their wings, or open them too often, and that would be it. Even the lower gravity of Henson's Tube doesn't let you make a mistake like that more than once. My father says he saw his best friend get killed opening up too late, and I remember how Keri started crying when Moody came plummeting down out of the air and we thought he'd never open his wings and glide.

Still, when you get to be a certain age in Henson's Tube, you go up the Endcap to the station and hitch a ride on the catchrails of the Shuttle. And when it gets to the middle of the cable, you jump off. It's not all that dangerous really if you open your wings at the right times. The way gravity works in Henson's Tube, or any of the other orbiting space colonies for that matter, makes it a lot less dangerous than doing the same thing on Earth.

The difference in gravity comes from the way Henson's Tube is shaped. It's like a test tube, sealed at both ends. The people all live on the inside walls of the tube, and the tube is spun, like an axle in place, to give it gravity. If you look with a pair of Close-ups, you can see land overhead above the clouds, but the other side of the Tube is five kilometers away, and that's a long way when it's straight up.

If you were born in the Tube like we all were, it doesn't seem unnatural to you to be spun around continually in two-minute circles, and even tourists find it just like Earth, all rocks and trees and stuff, until they look up. Of course, the one-half gravity at "ground level" makes them a little nervous, but the real difference in gravity is at the center of the Tube. There's a sort of invisible axle running down the center of the tube lengthwise, where there's no gravity. That's where the Shuttle runs on its cable from one Endcap to the other. And that's where you start your Fall.

You step off the Shuttle halfway along its ride, and you drift very slowly toward one side of the Tube. But pretty soon the ground rotates away, under you, and the wind begins to push you around the center cable too. Only you don't just go around it in a circle, because going around starts giving you some gravity, so you come spiraling down toward the ground, rotating always a bit slower than the Tube itself.

The closer you get to the sides, the faster the Tube—the ground—spins on past you. The gravity depends on how much you've caught up with the rotating of the Tube. If you didn't have wings, you'd hit hard enough to get killed for sure, partly from falling and partly because the ground would be going past so fast when you hit. If you do have wings, then they slow down your falling okay, but then they catch the wind more, so you're rotating almost as fast as the Tube is. Only then, because you're going around faster, the gravity is stronger and you have to really use the wings to keep from landing too hard. Only by then you're probably halfway around the Tube from where you wanted to land, and it's a long walk home.

Usually, you just step off the Shuttle and drop with your wings folded until you get scared enough to open your arms. When you do, your wings begin to slow your fall. If you don't wait too long, that is. If you *do* wait too long, when you throw your arms open, they get snapped up and back like an umbrella blowing inside out, and there's nothing left to stop you. Most of the people who get hurt Skyfalling get scared and open their wings too soon or too often. Most of the ones who get killed open their wings too late. Nobody had ever seen Keri get scared.

That was probably what Moody was thinking about as he ran for the door. I know it was what I was thinking about as I grabbed a pair of Close-ups that must have been Keri's and ran after him. Lobber ran after both of us, shouting. By the time we got outside, the silver, bullet-shaped car of the Shuttle was about a third of the way along its cable, and there was nothing to do but wait until it got almost directly above us.

At first, we couldn't see Keri and we thought he must have missed the Shuttle, but then we saw him, sitting on the long catchrail on the underside of the Shuttle with his feet over the side. Lobber kept trying to grab my Close-ups, shouting, "Let me look! Let me look!" I ignored him, but it didn't do any good until Moody grabbed him and said "Shut up, Lobber, just shut up!" Lobber looked like he was going to start shouting about being told to shut up, but the Shuttle was almost directly overhead by then, so he did shut up and watched.

When the Shuttle got where he wanted it, Keri stood up, stopped for a second to pick out his landmarks and then just stepped off. He fell slowly at first, almost directly above us. But soon he began to slide back and away from us in wider and wider spirals as the Tube revolved. For a second, he looked like he was just standing there watching the Shuttle go on down the Tube and us slide away beneath him.

But in a couple seconds he went from being as big as my thumb to being as big as the palm of my hand. We could tell he was riding down the pull of gravity at a good speed and getting faster all the time. He had his head into the wind and his body out behind him to cut down his resistance, so the wind wasn't rotating him with it too much, and his speed was going up and up and we knew he'd have to do something soon to cut it down.

When he was half a mile above us, he still hadn't opened his wings. Moody lowered his Close-ups and shook his head like he was sure Keri would never make it. When he looked up again, Keri was a lot closer to the ground, and his blue wings were still folded across his chest. It's hard to tell from the ground how far you can fall before you pass the point where it's too late to open your wings, but it looked to us like Keri had already passed it. And he still hadn't spread his wings.

"Open up!" Moody shouted, "Open up!" And for a little while Keri did just that, until he began to slide back around the curve of the Tube. But long before he whould have, he pulled his arms back in and started that long dive again. All Lobber could see was a small fluttering fall of blue against the checkerboard of the far side of the Tube. "He's out of control!" Lobber shouted.

He was wrong, of course. For some crazy reason of his own, Keri had done it on purpose, but when I went to tell Lobber to shut up, I found that my mouth was too dry to talk. It didn't matter, because Lobber went suddenly quiet. Moody stood looking up through his Close-ups and muttering, "Open up, Keri! Open up!"

It seemed like an hour before Keri finally did. You could almost hear the flap of the blue fabric as he threw his arms open. His arms snapped back, and for a minute, I thought he was going to lose it, but he fought them forward and held them out steady.

But it still looked like he had waited too long. He was sliding back a little, but he was still falling, and falling fast. I could see him straining against the force of his fall, trying to overcome it, but I didn't think he was going to make it.

I didn't want to follow him in that long fall all the way into the ground. I thought about how my father said his friend had looked after he hit, and I knew I didn't want to see Keri like that. But just before I looked away, Keri did the craziest thing I ever saw. Falling head down with his arms out, he suddenly jack-knifed himself forward, held it for a second, then snapped his head up and spread-eagled himself. His wings popped like a billowbag opening up.

Moody gave a little gasp and I felt my own breath suck in. But it turned out that Keri knew more about Skyfalling than either of us ever would and when he threw his arms back, he had almost matched ground speed and the maneuver had put him into a stall so close to the ground that I still don't believe it was possible.

Of course, Keri being Keri, he held his wings out

just a fraction too long, and he went up and over before he could snap his arms down completely and came down backward. You could almost hear the crunch when he hit. I swear he bounced and flipped over backwards and then bounced and rolled over four more times before he stopped. For a second we just stood there, too stunned to move, and then we were suddenly all running toward him, with Moody in the lead.

When we got to Keri, he was sitting up, unsnapping his wings and rubbing his shoulders. His arms were a mess, all scraped and scratched, but not broken. Even though he had a helmet on, one eye was swollen shut. But he was smiling.

Moody got to him first and helped him up. "You're crazy, Keri! You know that?! You could have got yourself killed! You know that?! You know that?!" I don't think I ever remember Moody being that mad. He sounded like his father. "Look at you! You're lucky you didn't get killed!"

But Keri just kept grinning and the louder Moody got, the wider Keri grinned until Moody just turned away in disgust. Nobody said anything for a while, not even Lobber. Finally Keri said, "C'mon, Moody, I didn't act like that when *you* came down."

Moody turned around and looked at his brother like he knew Keri was right, but he wasn't ready yet to forgive him for scaring us like that. "Yeah, but I didn't wait until I almost hit the ground before I opened up! I didn't scare anybody half to death thinking I was going to get myself killed!"

Keri looked at him and chuckled. "Didn't you?"

"That wasn't the same!" Moody said. But you could tell he knew it was. Finally, he grabbed Keri's wings. "Here, give me those before you tear them."

Keri laughed and handed him the wings. He gave me a wink with his good eye. "Not easy being on the ground. Is it?" I shook my head. Moody just snorted and folded the wings. I kept waiting for Lobber to start shouting again, but he didn't. He just looked up at where the Shuttle had passed, and when he spoke, his voice was wistful and quiet like he knew Skyfalling was something he would never be able to do, no matter how much he might want to. "What does it feel like, Keri?" he said.

Keri shrugged, and I knew it was because there is something in the Fall, something about the way it gets faster and faster, and the ground rushes up at you like certain death, that he couldn't explain. I could see the freedom of it still sparkling in his eyes. "It feels like being alive."

TO SIN AGAINST SYSTEMS
by Garry R. Osgood

*Mr. Osgood was born about 24 years
ago in Suncook, NH. He got an E.E.
degree from New Hampshire Technical
Institute, led a patchwork career
in small-town newspaper publishing
(he even edited a paper for a short
while and reports he hasn't recovered
yet), and now attends Cooper Union.
He's a cybernetic nut, with a
particular interest in applying
micro-computers to games. This
story is his first fiction sale.*

With a defiant squeak, the chalk finished its last block diagram for the year while I concluded to the blackboard, "So the classical tube amplifier can be represented by the block μ times the load resistor, R_L plus the internal plate resistance r_P. This transfer function represents the ideal gain of the system and relates the time varying function at the block's input port to the output function."

I turned to the young faces of the class and pitched the chalk stub in the wastepaper basket. The classroom was hot. My shirt was sticking to my back, and I had beads of perspiration growing on my forehead. There was one last hurdle between these kids and the summer vacation.

"The final for this course will be held in the lecture hall L-212, I guess." I peered at the assignment sheet posted on the bulletin board, to keep up the appearance that I was myopic. "On Friday, first period— nice and early in the morning." Nobody laughed. I sat down on the desk and mulled over the various bits of wisdom that a professor should pass on to his departing students. There were damn few items that weren't already stale. I rubbed my chin, peered out the window, and decided on a few classics.

"Everybody should bring a pencil, I guess. A school that can't afford individual terminals probably can't afford pencils—or a sharpener, so bring a spare." That was classic enough, so I left them with some personal philosophy: "I think if you go into this thing with the idea of memorizing a lot of equations, you'll run into a great deal of trouble. Remember the underlying concepts, the reasons why the equations are written the way they are. We are dealing with integrated and inter-related systems here, and not discrete pieces. Nowhere in the exam are you given equations. You are given a system. Take the overview approach and look at the system as a whole, and the proper relations will suggest themselves if you don't bury yourself in minute and unimportant aspects."

Well, that's what all engineering profs say anyway, so I guess I didn't add anything new to student lore.

"See you next year—some of you. Get lost." And away they went. Some were intent and some were asleep; I wondered if teachers were ever any use. Chances were I wouldn't be seeing them again next year, anyway. I was feeling the weather in my joints, and I didn't like getting up in the morning anymore. Both were signs that soon I would have to hole up somewhere and go through a metamorphosis. I didn't think that I could leave it for another year; and after it was done I would have to be someone else—two lifetimes of Professor Gilbert Fenton were more than I could take. It had been fun for a while, teaching these kids; but the subject matter was getting stale of late. I had taught it too many times. I'd be doing myself and these kids a favor if I became somebody else.

I walked out of the old ivy-covered brick building into the heat of a midwestern day in May. I found myself wandering down a shady, sleepy walk of American academe. It was one of those late spring days that whisper, like the wind through the trees, "Summer is here." The students who had doubts about their futures were hitting the books and typewriters for their final papers and whatnots. Those who were in no doubt—the 'smart' and the otherwise—were infesting the beer halls and hangouts of the college town.

It had been my pleasure to have for the last few days a companion, of sorts, though I knew neither who he was nor where he came from. I hadn't even spoken with him. He was a slender youth, dressed in the standard uniform of T-shirt and jeans. He didn't amount to anything save for those eyes of his. He had first caught my attention, then my curiosity. As I turned the corner of the lane on that sleepy summer day, my companion of sorts saw me; upon seeing me, he propelled himself down the street like the boy who had made the acquaintance of the preacher's daughter and the sheriff; the latter being an unplanned circumstance. Seeing him struck me as a very curious thing, for apparently I had gone through most of the year without noticing him; and when I finally did I couldn't avoid him. This sometimes happens with me: to be aware of people is to see them; but I don't think I would have noticed this particular youth in the first place if it had not been for those eyes. He reminded me of a friend; Sheridan had eyes like that youth: steel grey eyes that penetrated and calculated, windows to a sharp intellect. Sheridan was a living embodiment of von Neumann's ideal game player: perfectly intelligent and perfectly ruthless. In all my years he has been the only one to really guess who I am.

Damn him.

While I have lain low in life, Sheridan always grabbed the limelight, always wanted still more; though age was slowing him down at last. He and I first met in a rooming house on Fulton Street in New York City, in the year 1912. He was a lad of twenty and I . . . well I was passing through, in need of folding money or a man who was handy with a printing press. Sheridan had both. But he was also a most perceptive lad, and he picked up something that had kept him on my trail ever since. I considered the memory. It has been ninety years since I made that acquaintance. Sheridan was now very old, and very rich—and very persistent. I decided that I might just put old Gilbert Fenton to rest that night; Sheridan's grey eyes might run in the family. After I metamorphose I generally make myself quite different and turn up quite far from where I start, and Sheridan usually loses me for a spell. If I pulled the dodge one more time, I probably wouldn't have to worry again. I set off with decision in my step, light-hearted, in a way; I was about to begin again.

Perhaps I shouldn't be harsh on Sheridan, though. For all that I abhor his fascination with wealth and power, I haven't come one iota closer to the Universal Why than he has: which is to say, not at all. I have been looking for some time, too. I recalled, as I walked down the lane, That Woman—metamorphosing always makes me nostalgic—she had had an insight that impressed me deeply. She was old—mentally old—for an ephemeral. I had thought that with two of us on the job, the Universal Why wouldn't be too hard to find, so on her eightieth birthday I gave her the insight I have been able to exercise on myself as a gift to celebrate our fifty-five-year-old friendship. Afterwards, she was very quiet; and some time later she found the Universal Why at the bottom of a mine shaft. I was very thoughtful about the matter of self-annihilation after that, and I swore that I would understand a human being *thoroughly* before I tried the stunt again. I started the new policy with myself, and I'm still working with the first candidate.

You can understand how thoughtful a man becomes when considering such terribly human matters. That day I should have been careful. I am not immortal: I am a well-tuned mechanism, granted, but I can break. I should have paid attention to the crunch of gravel on the road as the car coasted along in neutral, the engine off. The car came alongside me (lost as I was in fond reverie), and a door opened.

"Hey, Bill! Wanna ride?"

Well, it wasn't my name but I looked up anyway. The youth with steel grey eyes was adding sounds of plausibility to what amounted to a kidnapping—though I was far too old to be a kid. I felt a little twinge of pain and a mild feeling of regret. A quick investigation of my chemical systems told me that the sedative was fast-acting and already rooted in too many places for me to whip up an effective counteragent.

Shucks. Can't win 'em all.

They were gentle with me. I suspect they all had hospital experience; Sheridan knew how to pick his staff. I was sure I was going to see him again. I can't call him friend, but it's people like him who make the world go round the way it does: sadly.

§ § §

The ride up to the Polar Orbital Station, administrative offices of The Sheridan Group Industries, was uneventful. I'd have been drugged to the gills if I had any.

It was a peaceful awakening, considering the abruptness of my abduction. I found myself in a nice, soft bed in a room of pastel colors. In the background there was the rustle of pink noise, which at one moment suggested the wind through tree branches, at another, the dance of water through rocks. I had the warm feeling that follows a good long sleep, but I was not at all sure how this next meeting with Sheridan would go. I looked for a clock but couldn't find one. I sat back on my pillows with the vague disquiet that comes when I'm completely disoriented in time. I don't think the temporal displacement would have been all that bad, if I hadn't found that I had company.

A male steward. A large male steward. Rather larger than four of me in fact.

I gave him what I imagined was a glower but it didn't seem to scare him.

"Hey, Shorty. How about telling your Boss that I'm awake?" I said.

He looked over his shoulder at me, uncrossed his arms from behind his back, turned, bowed curtly. From anyone else, the gesture would have looked ridiculous, but he gave it an air of poetry; and besides, he was bigger than I, so I didn't laugh. Through his smile he said,

"Mr. Sheridan will be with you presently. In the meantime, if there is anything that I can do—"

"Leave," I suggested.

"That would not be possible, I'm afraid." A smile, a bow. I rapped out a few drum rolls with my fingers and thought a few thoughts.

"Hmm. Can you dance? Do magic tricks? How

about some clothes? Sure as taxes your Boss man is going to chew the fat with me eventually." Why else would he go to all this trouble?

"Certainly." He snapped his fingers, and another version of him, somewhat smaller perhaps, appeared. This didn't help, I thought. It wasn't that I wanted privacy so I could escape—where could I escape to, on Sheridan's own orbital satellite? I didn't think they'd lend me a shuttle; assuming I could find a shuttle, assuming I could run a shuttle, or assuming that I could go through the bang, bang, shoot-'em-up heroics that would be required to get one. I haven't lived since A.D. 900 by giving people excuses to shoot at me. I wanted privacy because I was prudish, and if I asked for anything else, I'd probably get a brass band to watch me dress.

"How 'bout some privacy? You expect me to dress to an audience?" They both complied. In unison they turned their backs. The choreography was superb.

I knew Sheridan was well off, but I began to wonder if even that could adequately describe a man who owned his own space station. When I first met him he was just another two-bit waterfront chiseler with an accommodating smile and a printing press that spit out sawbucks and fins. On the side he could do magic with a piece of paper. He could match stock certificates to inks and to presses. He could take a document from any institution and turn out a very reasonable facsimile lickety-split.

At the time, the various patrons I served in the booking industry were tossing those significant glances my way that told me that it was time to move on, and like Tammany Hall, I did. I picked Sheridan because I needed the various bits of paper naming an individual to be crisp and well done. Sheridan was just a kid, but he was beginning to get the reputation of being a phenomenally skilled kid. True to form, he was thorough with his patrons and kept an eye on me even after I thought I had finished doing business with him. My thirteenth metamorphosis had had a cheering section.

The togs fit perfectly. One of the goons brought me a mirror, and I saw that I liked the cut and style of the clothes. Warm color, simple, with no baroque frills. Sheridan remembered my tastes and had gained some skill on the soft pedal. It was very different from the techniques that he used on me before; the last time we met, Sheridan caressed me with an india rubber hose.

He has had a long time to learn, I reflected. Sheridan must be at least a hundred and ten, and still a captain of industry. He should have become an honorary member of the Board of the Sheridan Group Industries forty years ago, but he didn't retire. He still had enough energy to secure his position in the business and chase me all over India, when he got wind of me there. I looked around the compartment. It was well appointed. I could have been on the Terran surface. Sheridan was a scoundrel who would sell his mother down the river; but he was a capable, intelligent, and gifted scoundrel. One of the goons cleared the ceiling and I amused myself by watching the activity on the Station's Hub.

In a short while I heard the door mechanism. The two goons got up to go as the compartment door slid quietly into the bulkhead.

It was Sheridan.

Oh, he was old, and very thin, but I couldn't make the word 'frail' hang on him. His was the distinguished kind of old that one associates with the occupants of stone castles, who cultivate very fine wines. His back was straight. He was neat as a pin, and though his cheeks were sunken he still had the hawk nose and the penetrating, steel grey eyes. I had the urge to stand up in his presence, to forget about the abduction and the rubber hose: he had an atmosphere of command just like that. I almost got up—but I didn't.

"Good afternoon—Gilbert, is it?" he asked, and held out a hand that I didn't take. He had a nice, rich voice, with just a slight trace of a piping waver. Ordinarily, I would like a man with a voice like that.

I scratched my head, still sprawled out on the bed, looked up at the Hub, and said it was as good a name as any. "Is it afternoon? Heck, Pappy, I should be hungry now. Got anything to eat in this oversized bicycle wheel?"

"'Afternoon' by Greenwich Mean. I suspect it would be early in the morning in Midwestern America. You either will, or already have notified the college that you have been taken ill."

"Thanks, Pappy, I guess. You always were thorough." The last time we had met he had been a near youngster, and I'd been apparently in my late seventies. I wasn't a youngster at the moment, but the apparent age-spread between us was the same, only the sign had been changed.

"Chester," he addressed one of the goons by the door, "attend to dinner for Mr. Fenton and myself. Have it served in the Observatory. After that, you and the staff shall retire from my living quarters until 0800 tomorrow."

"Very good, Mr. Sheridan." Chester and the other goon left in a butlerish sort of way.

Sheridan turned his attention back to me, saying, "To the Observatory, sir? The view of the Earth is magnificent—Olympian, even."

"As beheld by an Olympian god, perhaps?" I asked.

Sheridan smiled, ignored my sally and asked: "Have you ever seen the Earth from this vantage point?"

"Naw," I replied. "This is a first. First time in orbit, too. Can't say that it's much different from any Terran flophouse—purtier, maybe."

Sheridan allowed a calculated degree of surprise. "The first time? I thought that you had the time to try everything." Sheridan arched his eyebrows just so.

"What? Impossible. Sir, I have just begun!" I replied.

"... And at an age when most men have long retired from their affairs," Sheridan added. Then he cocked his eyebrow and fixed me with a steely sidelong glance. "Except that it's 'all men' in your case, Gilbert?"

"Speak for yourself, Chief," I retorted. "You aren't doing too badly either. Banging around in orbit. Hell, you got your start out of the backside of a horse-drawn wagon. Are you telling me that you've finally figured it out for yourself and you don't need my services?"

"Business after lunch, Fenton. We old fellows shouldn't rush about. Let us say I have changed my mind on certain fundamental points in our century-old cat-and-mouse game."

"You've decided to be the mouse?" I asked with staged surprise.

"Maybe, Fenton, I have been the mouse all along. Quiet, now." We had been riding in a slidevator that ran along the rim of the Station. It had reached its last stop, and the doors slid open. Sheridan guided

me to another set of double doors. With his finger poised over the opening plate, he turned to me and whispered: "Hold on; this view will take your breath away. I've had people faint here."

The doors opened into an oval room with dark walls and unobtrusive lights scattered about the ceiling. Save for small islands and threadlike catwalks, the floor opened out into parsecs of inky black space, scattershot with points of light. The Milky Way was drifting with stately dignity beneath our feet.

"Walk out onto it. The floor is quite an engineering feat itself."

And I saw Earthrise at the Polar Orbital Station.

Moving with a graceful pace, Northern Europe hove into view, dressed in the satin white lace of a fair-weather system. To my left, protracted, was the North American continent, glowing under a late morning sun. White and sapphire, russet and green, Terra spun slowly against a velvet backdrop; and behind her, the Milky Way drifted in the vastness of the expanding Universe. I was awestruck, thunderstruck, and struck by a million items so vanishingly small, yet so brilliantly resolved: the sun's highlight on the Atlantic, individual textures of clouds, the incredibly involved texture of the land. If ever I had a feel for the comprehension of the Universal Whole, it was in that Observatory.

I wasn't going to fall . . . but I wasn't going to let go of Sheridan, either.

"Sher—Sheridan?"

"Sir."

"I'm impressed. Where can I sit down?"

Sheridan helped me along the walk, over the Mid-Atlantic, and sat me down at a table somewhere above the Ural Mountains. For some time I had forgotten to breathe. I checked my pulse, spent some minutes doing something about all the adrenalin my glands had so thoughtlessly dumped into my bloodstream, and soothed senses that *swore* I was going to fall out of the place. There were a number of body-keeping chores that I had to attend to right there.

"Do you have a fear of heights?" Sheridan asked pleasantly.

"Only—recently, Sheridan. I didn't think they could make a transparent shield of such dimensions."

"Anything can be done with money, Gilbert. The costs of developing the Observatory were indeed high, but you should see the effect it has on the stockholders. Between you and me and the Board, the principal stockholders require little additional conditioning after they've been in this room. They respond to this place as they would to a religious experience; indeed, for some it's the only religious experience they ever have."

Conditioned stockholders. A typical Sheridan scheme. But, I had to admit to myself, I hadn't been moved like this since I was sixteen and inside my first cathedral. Life was more carefree then; I didn't have to trouble myself with the schemings of old men—or escaping from their space stations to protect the secret of longevity. For all its faults, the world didn't deserve an immortal Sheridan.

I think Sheridan felt embarrassed in the silence that followed his remark. I peered at him in the green and blue earthlight, and he fumbled with his fingers and then burst out: "Oh, the conditioning isn't that severe! We have no use for a bunch of Pavlov dogs! The conditioning is very subtle, and actually falls into that never-never land between conditioning, convincing, and educating. They aren't even aware of it. The only form it takes is the inclination to invest in one kind of a scheme, every now and then, rather than another; and to keep re-electing the present Board of Directors and myself. That's hardly dictating their every movement! And we're only dealing with one-thousandth of one percent of the world's population."

"The ones with money," I said, levelly.

"Well, that is hardly an abuse of power," he said,

forcing conviction into his voice.

"Did I sound like I was objecting?" I asked.

"Oh . . ." Sheridan seemed surprised. Poor fella; he was warming up to a justification speech that he found out he didn't need. He didn't know what to do with his mouth—and I felt good. At least for that instant he wasn't in the driver's seat!

"I rather thought you would," he said, a little lamely. "You always were a liberal moralist, Gilbert. You objected to the printing of bogus money even as you were accepting your degree from—'Matheus University'? I think that was the place I gave you." I got a thin smile as soft sounds from the ramp announced Chester's arrival with the chow.

Chester was unimpressed by the spectacle beneath his feet. The green-blue light from the floor lit him up like an apparition from the Ektachrome of a bad horror movie.

I replied to Sheridan's comment, "Times change; so do the opinions of cantankerous old men."

Sheridan nodded thoughtfully. He began to cut carefully into the steak. Since my background lacked grace and form, I attacked my portion in the spirit of an Apache raid on an intruding wagon train.

In time I asked through the music of utensils on porcelain, "So, Pappy; how's the printing business?"

Sheridan stopped the elegant business of eating. He looked at me and tried to gauge any hidden meaning in my question.

"I sold it to someone who could appreciate it. I purchased a bakery and sold it as a bread company. I bought into Rockwell International and recommenced the manufacture of the Shuttle when the energy depletion scare finally blew away. It was difficult, but men aren't all that difficult to control, if they are ambitious. You figure out what they want, and then you make them think you've delivered it to them—all for a price, mind you."

"Hmm," I said. He had suggested something to me . . . but what was it? A plan, a whole brazen plan flashed in front of me and—I lost it. My glimmer didn't reach the gleam stage.

Sheridan, asked, between bites, "And how are you proceeding, sir?"

As if he didn't know. "I've been trying my hand as an engineering prof in a diploma mill," I replied. "I have no illusions about the sanctity of the learning process. There are people who learn—and people who look for the instructions on things."

"Education, a personal process, what?"

"Yep." I launched my last piece of steak on its next phase of existence and said around the bite, "Maybe the process is easier in defined atmospheres, with research material and someone to help you who knows the ropes; but it's still a personal process. Maybe the word 'teacher' is meaningless. Maybe 'learning assistant' is better."

Chester was gone. We were alone now.

"I am going to make a proposition, Gilbert."

"Anything like the last one? As I recall, you presented it with a great deal of persistent vigor."

Sheridan laughed a polite laugh, which revealed a row of perfect teeth. The floor was opaquing in response to a local sunrise. "And I would have continued to do so if you hadn't found a door I didn't know existed."

That wasn't how I had gotten out; but if that was what he wanted to think, then I wasn't going to disillusion him.

Sheridan continued: "But you must admit that I have developed a great deal of sophistication since those days. Here we are in an orbital station, amid the offices and laboratories of the Sheridan Group Industries. A thousand office workers and technicians and their families reside here. No one knows you are here but you and I."

"What about Chester?"

"Chester? He thinks you're someone who has to be persuaded to do a little business. He has no idea that you are a millennium old or what you are here for.

He rather hopes to help out in a little accident that will occur in your local area if you can't be persuaded. But he shall be disappointed this time, fortunately."

"You mean you'd let me go if I didn't tell you how I do what I do?" I asked.

"I haven't planned what I'd do with you if you refused me," replied Sheridan, easily. I couldn't imagine a situation where Sheridan hadn't laid a plan for each detail. Sheridan was meticulous.

"You see," he said after a pause to consider his last piece of steak, "I am rather confident that we can come to an agreement, shall we say." Sheridan carefully arranged his silverware on his plate. "I considered that I might have to demonstrate to the authorities that you were never here, of course. Let us say that it comes to unpleasantness. Several people might swear that you were uncommonly careless in the traffic lanes near Des Moines, Iowa, say. But I don't intend to harm you. We are life-long companions, of sorts, equal gentlemen, you and I; and I have a proposition." He neatly swiped at his mouth with his napkin.

"Sheridan," I said warily, "I do not use the term 'gentleman' for someone who uses rubber hose diplomacy."

Sheridan winced and with a waving hand cleared the air of my ungentlemanly observation. "Oh, please don't say that. I've grown up, Fenton. At a hundred and ten I can see myself in perspective. I've come to realize that I am dependent on you for just a little flow of information. I can't beat you to death, you'd die with the secret and a smirk on your lips, I know. I'd be as badly off as I was before I brought you up here, worse because you'd be dead; and there isn't another man on the face of the Earth that knows what you know."

"Maybe. Folks like us are mighty particular with our identities."

"You mean there are *others* . . .?" Sheridan's expression told me I'd better can that line, or my life wouldn't be worth one of Sheridan's funny-money sawbucks.

"How the hell do I know? You've been looking around, have you found any?"

Sheridan looked bitter. "No, but I have you. A bird in hand. No, Gil, I was wrong to try to beat it out of you, though I wouldn't admit it at the time. I was extraordinarily lucky that I didn't kill you; for I was strong as an ox, and I had all the passion of youth. But then you were out that extra door, Gil, and I swore that someday I would be in a position to buy you, if I had to. In a way, you are responsible for Sheridan Group Industries; you are its prime mover. I merely gathered the resources to track you down."

"And now you've got all that dough and I'm not the least interested in it," I said tiredly. "I generally outlive the local currency standards. What is wealth then? If that's the basis of your proposition, to trade your future for your empire... You've bored me, Sheridan."

Sheridan pushed his empty plate back and rose from his chair. He began to pace the floor, now fully occluded and pearly white from the attenuated sunlight.

"No, Gil. I could offer you lifelong wealth as a part of the commission, which for you would be quite a pile, but that is not my intention. Gil, my proposition is that I won't pay you a red cent. I'll pay Humanity."

I smiled. Deathbed morality catches up with the richest man in the world. "Do tell, I say."

"Gil, I know you want a better Humanity. Beneath your cynicism you want every person to live better and far longer. Maybe you want them to live indefinitely. Am I right?"

I shrugged, suppressing a thrill of wonder. "Has he changed?" I asked myself, then a mental chuckle realigned the errant neurons.

"That what all right-thinking people on the globe want—for the record. Have you got something concrete to back up those pleasant words?" I smiled and watched him pace to my side of the table.

"I have been amassing wealth, Gil; but more important, I have been amassing *control*.

"Fact:" announced Sheridan. "Since the depression that preceded World War II, and in a larger sense since the Industrial Revolution, the gross economic trend has been the concentration of wealth into the hands of a smaller and smaller circle of people and institutions. At first it was direct personal wealth. Personal wealth purchases goods and services—and money is purchasable, like beer and pickles. Hence we have people who sell money, for profit; they rent out a commodity that won't wear out and is guaranteed by the governments of the world. Since the members of the service class are wealthy to start with, they become wealthier—"

"Positive feedback," I said.

"Eh?"

"Positive feedback. Like a feedback circuit where the linkage is multiplicative with a positive sign at the circuit's summation point. The output shows an exponential change in magnitude to the limits of the supply, or it steals wind from other supplies."

Sheridan seemed to like the engineering. He beamed, "An essentially similar viewpoint, Gil. I didn't think you had it in you.

"Anyway, there is a tendency for wealth to concentrate. To control the concentrations of wealth is to have that wealth, and the power it represents, in your hands. My strategy for the last sixty years has been to allow other people's wealth to accumulate, so I can then take control of it. I have not been troubled by the politics of the masses.

"Now, what to do with that power? One can purchase or develop technological means to control people who control wealth. Right hemisphere implants—a crude method—chemotherapy via food doping, non-volitional conditioning. . ." He paused. "Anyway, we've developed many techniques here at the Station. Fact. Sheridan Group Industries can now control the purchasing and investment habits of twenty-five percent of the pivotal individuals and institutions."

I shrugged. Sheridan was getting excited in the pearly sunlight. "So? You've dedicated a century of living to get control, but you're dying just the same. Tell me, Sheridan, what's the point? I'd really like to know—I've got a hunch that civilization is a circus we've all put on to keep our minds off the main question: 'What happens after I shoot through . . ?'"

"That doesn't have to be the point. I represent a potential that has never existed before. I represent the apex of economic control. I can devastate the world economy by changing the value of paper tokens, simply by launching a series of booms, which trigger the busts. I can make the system oscillate wildly; I can destroy the links between the economic communities: people will go back to direct barter. Or, I can make the system work better because I can control enough of the system to reroute it—to improve it. That's a much harder trick; for it takes knowledge, experience, control—and *time*. There have been people like me before, but they gained the first three elements at the expense of the fourth, and whatever potential they had was cut off by the vanishingly small time they had left to use it in.

"Gil, you represent that fourth element, and I represent the other three. All four elements in one man, Gil; it would be tremendous." Sheridan waited, hesitant, expecting a reaction.

"Who gets the four elements?"

"I do, Gil. You give me the fourth element."

"And what's in it for me?"

"Nothing, Gil. There's nothing in it for you. I can't buy you a whore or bribe you with money, and at one time that annoyed me. But I've learned that I can rely on your higher principles. Trust me and give me longevity, and I'll use the time, control, knowledge and experience to pass that longevity on to humanity. I have the tools to do it.

"I'm not Pappy the Printer anymore. Diligence and unorthodox financial techniques have brought me to the brink of economic domination of the world. As I've watched this globe wheel beneath my feet, Gil, I've gained an understanding of what could be done. It'll take several years to re-tune the global economy to tolerate longevity, of course. I know what needs to be done. But I'll be dead before I can do it. I have the vision; Gil: give me the *time*."

The opalescent half-light sharpened to needle points as the floor cleared to reveal again the timeless Milky Way. Sheridan waited. He had spoken his piece.

Three seconds brought me almost—but not quite—to the conclusion that Sheridan was full of that elegant stuff that fills a soul while the body is on Death Row and that he would revert to his old foolishness if he got a pardon. Let us say that I was ninety percent sure of this. But as I am damned to see every side to a circular question, I was ten percent in doubt now and would be more than ten percent doubtful later and—*damn!*—I would most assuredly have to kill Sheridan if I didn't join him. What an awesome decision. My killing Sheridan, my being his executioner, could result only from an act of judgment. I have fundamental reservations about executing a man I haven't properly judged; to do so is to send him to that state that I have not yet had the courage to face myself.

Troubled, I tabled the thought. I said into the utter silence of that room, "Thank you."

"Eh?" was Sheridan's response.

"You are the first man who has tried to appeal to me with neither a sexy kitten nor a pile of gold. Instead, you've appealed to my morals. I thank you for the compliment."

Sheridan nodded tiredly. "I need what you have

but there is nothing in the world that I can give you in trade. So I'll tell you of my purpose and I ask you to judge if it's worthy one. I am completely dependent upon your believing me. I ask you to trust me, Gil, to judge me; to let me work, or to condemn me and watch me die." Still holding at ten percent, I thought.

But to have civilization on a leash! What a heady thought. And Sheridan had what it took. Almost. "What if I . . . don't decide immediately?"

"Wait," he answered. "I won't let you go, until you have decided; I think you owe me that.

"And if I . . . never decide?" I asked.

Sheridan played with his fork, smiled a bitter smile, and looked directly at me.

"Why," he said, "that would be the same as judging against me, wouldn't it?" He paused. "I've been dodging it for some time. We've used some pretty powerful techniques to keep me alive. I've made it to a hundred and ten; but the repair rate is getting out of hand. The doctor thinks I can live six more months." And Sheridan looked at me with twinkling, intelligent, predatory eyes.

"I think you had better prepare your guest room, Pappy."

"I'm not Pappy anymore. His attitude is dead."

"So he says."

"You'll see," said Sheridan, unruffled. "I can wait— for a little while. In the meantime, we'll need to keep you occupied. You'll be my personal assistant."

Sheridan and I walked through his personal section of the Station—two of the twenty-four major compartments circling the rim. The interior was decorated in subtle whites and greys, with curved floors, plants, sculpture, and paintings scattered about. One compartment was a guest area, which contained along with a get-together room, visiting quarters and servants' area, the Observatory. The other compartment was Sheridan's *sanctum sanctorum.* Sheridan led me past its locked door and into a wide room tastefully done in the same white and grey décor. In one corner of the main room, a terminal to the Station's library silently presented a menu of games and reading material. Sheridan watched me while I browsed through some of the 1-person games, happy as a clam. Then he switched the terminal to the novice mode and showed me the query generator, commenting that this was one of the only two unsealed terminals in the Station, the other being in his room. "Look at anything you want," he said. "My life's work is on line." He then retired for the evening while I amused myself with the terminal.

I quickly discovered that the station library, and the station itself, were manifestations of Sheridan's interests. The station was his 'activity module', I suppose the best word is that; his library showed a preponderance of sociology, psychology, and biology, with an impressive number of unpublished papers. Sheridan had been gunning for the Fountain of Youth for some time, it seemed. A lot of his inquiries concerned genetic engineering—a practice banned on the surface—and he had on his staff Dr. William Vonner, who had gone into hiding when the scientific community announced its self-imposed moratorium on the design and manufacture of new species. It was good to know how the Doctor was biding his time.

A few touches of the paging stud informed me that Sheridan, while prospecting for the Fountain of Youth, had come up with a swarm of useful techniques. He had put brain implants and gene doping on a practical basis, if I interpreted this three-year-old report correctly, and had developed a system of protein fabrication that fit learning into little pills. He had been using it to teach languages to his staff and 'investment techniques' to clients who subscribed to his service. I whistled in appreciation: not only did Sheridan control his investors, they were paying for the privilege! He would have been a hell of a horse trader, back when.

After two hours at the data bank I sat back,

amazed. Sheridan's inquiries into the science of direct and indirect control of the human subject were the most exhaustive I had ever seen. He had hit the problem on both the macro and micro levels. He was developing a mathematics of n-dimensional topological spaces, and investigating how a functional projection of degree $(n-1)$ onto a given topological space could serve as a model for various macro-phenomena—how a crowd will sell, or buy, or revolt. On the micro level he was developing subtle methods of direct individual control like his 'subscription service.'

The man had no competition in the science of manipulation. With all of these control mechanisms at his command, he could have become dictator of the Earth in the most subtle way, and no one would have been particularly aware of it—

I jerked up.

Maybe he was now. Maybe he just needed me to assure his subsequent terms in office.

Or maybe he was still consolidating his position and treading water until he was sure he could direct all phases of the program personally, without having to be inconvenienced halfway through by dropping dead.

Or maybe deathbed morality had changed his reach, redirected his vision, and he was waiting for me to give him the go-ahead, the time to do the world right—the world he had so sorely cheated. The groundwork was there for something magnificent, shenanigans or otherwise.

I turned off the terminal, stretched out on the resilient floor, and threw a pillow over my head.

I had, I thought, a powerful investigative tool that would clear out a lot of the guesswork—the longevity therapy itself. I discovered shortly after my first metamorphosis that I could gain access to other people's minds if they 'let me in'. The process is a little more complicated than that, but that is the best I can do with the language. Once I was let in I had a wide communication spectrum with a subject, and I could see—Hell, it isn't 'see' but that's the best word going—I could see his neural network and his chemical systems as well as he could; better, because I knew where to 'look' and he didn't. Telepathy and this clear inner eye and control of one's inner processes seem to go hand in hand and indeed, might even be the same phenomenon. I could learn a lot about what really went on in Sheridan's mind during the initial rapport, and I could pull out if I saw anything I did not like. If he were being totally deceptive he might even balk at a telepathic link-up, and my decision would be easy—though getting out of the station might be pretty hard. I rather liked that alternative. I took off the pillow and smiled to myself. There just might be a way out.

I slept on the problem until a female voice by my head said, "Mr. Sheridan asked me to remind you that it is 0600, and that you are to meet with him at 0700 in the Administration Compound, segment zero one hundred, room thirteen."

"Fair 'nuff," I muttered. I wandered into the bathroom, and cycled the refresher cube until I was reasonably awake. Breakfast was a problem, and fresh clothing; and I pondered the point in my birthday suit until I remembered the terminal. I negotiated a large breakfast and a small wardrobe; in two minutes a chime rang out and I had what I'd asked for, although the surrogate coffee needed some development work.

I headed to work on my first job with the great Mr. Sheridan.

I found segment zero one hundred between zero two hundred and two four hundred. A 'can you tell me where Mr. Sheridan's office is?' got me the rest of the way.

"Good morning!" greeted Sheridan.

"It'll be a while before I have an opinion on it," I replied. He smiled. "I've got a job for you. Come with me, I'm starting on my rounds." We went through a priest's hole and into some unlisted corridor.

"The thing, is I'm getting forgetful in my old age," he said. "Every day I walk around to all of the departments and see the heads, trade a few words with the help. There are over a thousand people employed here, Fenton; and I know all of their names and faces—and all about their wives, husbands, lovers, families, and kids too. I used to remember all the things they told me, important or not. People work better for me when they think I care about them."

I nodded.

"But as I said, I'm getting forgetful, so I'd like you to tag along and keep track of things for me."

"Besides, you would always have your eye on me," I said.

"There's that too, isn't there," agreed Sheridan. "Of course, if you find the job offensive, I can always find another one for you. Engineering is a forte of yours. I have some systems work—"

"No, no. Don't go to a lot of trouble," I said. "I just might want to keep an eye on you too."

"Ha! Fenton, if life were any different, we just might have been friends—we still could be. But I must ask you to be quiet, and careful as to what you say, for on the other side of these doors are the public corridors."

The large doors slid easily in their slots to reveal a businesslike corridor. To the left, at various intervals, were the slidevator stations; to the right were the working spaces appropriate for the pinnacle of the Sheridan Group Industries.

We went into a bio lab.

Some people, working at individual terminals, looked up. Sheridan got a chorus of 'Good Morning, Mr. Sheridan' and a few 'Hi Sher's.

"Morning, crew. Is Bill around?"

"In the office, Chief."

"Thanks, Frank. Group, I'd like you to meet Gil, my new memory man. If it's important, tell him. Gil is going to be the fellow who tells me what to do from now on."

Sheridan plowed to a hubward compartment, with me in tow.

The compartment was well laid out. There were happy plants all over the place, gentle curves, and light colors. We found the occupant contemplating the hub with a ghost of a smile on his lips.

"Good Morning, Dr. Vonner," said Sheridan. I arched my eyebrows.

"Hi, Sher. I've got a biggie," announced Bill as he swung his feet to the floor. There was enthusiasm in his eyes, a sheaf of papers in his hand. He was young, sandy haired and pudgy, late of the genetic engineering effort on the surface.

"Look at this, Sher: a definitive carrier loop that can modulate codon transfer during the pre-meiotic stage . . ."

And off he went, bubbling, enthusiastic, optimistic: a delighted child who had just learned a new magic trick. I could have been happy for him if I weren't so busy taking notes.

After about fifteen minutes, Vonner wound down and Sheridan was nodding thoughtfully. He handed back the sheaf to Vonner and said, "If you think you can control a mutation like that without radiation, Bill, then be my guest. Just don't let a hairy monster out into the lab."

"Hairy monster?" Vonner looked indignant. "I happen to be careful with my facilities—not like those jackasses on the surface, who probably wash their equipment in the nearest stream. Anything that I make will be so weak that it will self-destruct if I look at it cross-eyed."

Sheridan's bantering tone vanished. "I know you're careful, Bill. I'm basically conservative, that's all."

Vonner cooled off and his enthusiasm resurfaced. "You'll see the most wonderful things from this! History will be made in these labs!"

"I'd say you've made history in these labs already,

Bill. When we release some of your experiments to a—more understanding world, your name will rank with Salk and Pasteur."

Sheridan wheeled out of the office, leaving Vonner in a happy, creative flush. Before we got any distance, I had notes on two birthdays and an anniversary, along with two get-well cards.

When we got to the slidevator, Sheridan was in a thoughtful mood. He said, in part to himself, "You know, Vonner's lucky that he's up here. If his own safeguards fail, and worse comes to worse, there is always the ultimate safeguard."

"Such as?" I asked. Sheridan looked up at me.

"Oh! Well, Space itself. Genetic labs are ideally suited to orbit because that big old vacuum out there will get anything the radiation misses. If something—unpleasant—does happen up here, then I have deadman instructions controlling a nuclear device located in the Hub. Couldn't have that kind of safeguard anywhere on the surface."

"How about traffic to and from the Station between the time a bug gets loose and when the first symptoms show up?" I asked.

Sheridan looked surprised. "I *am* getting senile! Note somewhere on that pad that I should issue a general three-week quarantine on personnel leaving the Station. Call it General Instruction Q3. The Station Provost Officer is going to inundate me with grievances by tomorrow night, dollars to donuts."

Sheridan fell to inspecting his tightly cropped fingernails. I had a doomsday thought.

"Sheridan, suppose there is a plague in the near future, after you and I resolve our . . . differences," I asked, "would you blow yourself up with the Station?"

Sheridan fixed me with his eyes, his steely glinting eyes.

"I have you thinking about it, haven't I?"

"Maybe."

"You're thinking about it. Progress, I can't com-

206

plain." Sheridan sat back and a relieved expression crossed his face.

"Would you blow yourself up if the Incurable X disease slipped out of Vonner's test tube?" I pushed the matter. It was important.

The slidevator had stopped at the next station. Sheridan kept his bony fingers on the HOLD and DOOR CLOSE buttons, and said in a soft voice, tight with tension: "I have told you not to talk about this matter in public places. I suspect you made your way through the Black Plague in a manner that the contemporary alchemists would have found amazing, not to mention the present ones. It turns on what you teach me, Gil. Now *can it!*" The door opened and a perfectly composed Sheridan slipped out with a thoughtful memory man padding along behind.

There were sixteen anniversaries, two-score birthdays, ten get-well cards and thirty pages of notes from Sheridan to others via my aching fingers. My feet were killing me. Sheridan was just starting his day. I saw data processing and genetic experiments, high vacuum industrial experiments, and crystal-growing experiments, and I had notes to get data sheets on a dozen more.

"We do a lot of research here," remarked Sheridan as we headed back to his office. "This is the only private industrial facility in orbit, and we have clients who need testing done in the high vacuum and zero-g—plus all of the housework from the industries in the Group."

When we got into his office I gave him the note pad. Sheridan looked at my tight notes, diagrams, circles, arrows, and three-colored inserts and made a tsk, tsk, sound.

"Good heavens, Fenton, do you think the way that you write notes?"

I marveled, as I wriggled in my seat, how a fellow barely a century old could make me, with my ten centuries' seniority, feel like a junior office boy.

"This is the most amazing aggregation of mixed-up

markings... Here." Sheridan opened a drawer, exactly the one he wanted; reached in; and picked out a sealed metal cylinder. He snapped it open and rolled a large green pill onto his felt desk-top.

"Take it. It's a special shorthand that I can read and you can take, real-time, without looking at the notepad."

I looked dubiously at the pill, tapped my teeth with my pencil, and thought of that investment subscription service of his.

"Come on, I wouldn't poison you now, would I?" laughed Sheridan.

I was thinking of Vonner's enthusiasm—genuine human reaction or derived from a German language pill? Everyone that Sheridan dealt with was respectful, loyal, and even loving in a businesslike way. Was it love and respect on a human to human basis, or were they chemically treated dogs and yes-men?

I didn't know. It was all as enigmatic as Sheridan himself. But I knew my body chemistry and I had my inner 'eyes' and 'hands'. I made a bet with myself that I could nullify any chemical in that pill should it get out of hand. Swallowing it, I noted a slight suggestion of the taste/feel of dry peach rind, before the skin breaks. It was an interesting gamble, the kind that adds gusto to one's life. Besides, I was interested in how that pill would work on me.

"It'll be a while," remarked Sheridan. "Some of the secretaries say that when it starts to hit, it's best to draw some audio from the Station's library and practice. Others say to sleep on it. Do what comes naturally, and I'll see you tomorrow."

"Sure," I said, and I went to my quarters with my inner eyes watching.

§ § §

It was a pleasant inner show, that pill. It didn't touch my value areas one bit. Any fragment of protein that banged on the doors in that neighborhood got a gruff 'We don't want any'. The protein looked at its instructions, said, 'Excuse me!'

and moved on. When it got to the area that decided whether a sound should be shunted to a higher level or acted on right there, the proteins slipped in and established a correspondence between a sequence of motor instructions and phonal groups. The causality between 'loud noise: jump and cuss' which worked within a certain small loop suddenly had company in the form of such correspondences as 'freedom: motor instructions 4FEA'. There was a blocking neuron that controlled the loop, making it a function of will, so I wouldn't continually be urged to write everything I heard. When I *did* will the routine in, I would automatically write the shorthand analog of each word, knee-jerk fashion.

I suppose I could have done something similar myself, if I knew how; but there is a lot that I don't know about me. I do know the various control nexi and can manipulate a variety of neural, electrical, and chemical circuits. Since I see the body as a whole, I can appreciate the wide variety of 'domino chains' throughout the body: almost every circuit is linked to its neighbors, and an intentional adjustment will often trigger side effects in a (seemingly) unrelated function. Thus when I treat hardening of the arteries, I affect bone-cell manufacture. Though I know the nexi and how they can be excited, I still have to respect the overall body and its inter-related systems. In order for me to do that neural adjustment myself, I would be obliged to trace out all of the domino chains. Why Sheridan's little green pill failed to trigger any side effects is a mystery that goes to show how little I understand me, in spite of the intimate relationship that I enjoy with myself.

Which brought me to the problem of Sheridan, the next order of business after the Pill. My idea of what was on the man's mind and how it might be probed during the intimate link-up of the Therapy had taken a severe blow when I saw how Sheridan was received by his employees.

They liked him.

No one liked Sheridan when he was on Fulton Street. People did business with him because he was efficient, not because he was pleasant. Had he changed over the years?

Possibly Sheridan had changed. On the other hand, if it were deathbed morality, then I might miss it: unconscious self-deception, I cannot detect. I had missed That Woman's suicide tendency, and I was a hell of a lot more intimately bound to her than to Sheridan; and had rambled through her head for hours on end. And I now had the feeling that once I got inside of Sheridan, I would find answers that would beget more questions until it was *all* questions again.

In between arguing with myself, I watched the scenery that evening. The ceiling was cleared, and it treated me to alternate views of Space, then Earth, and then a period of occlusion while the sun was in view.

Good old Terra, I thought. Even she is a spaceship, with naturally evolving controls, hierarchies of systems, diverse phenomena working hand in hand: all of it fitting together so *right*. And the human creature is an outgrowth of that fit. Oh, he had a learning period, I thought, when he messed with chemicals that didn't dovetail with naturally existing systems; and when his material use was straight line, and not a loop that fed itself; but when the economics of recycling made themselves felt in the latter half of the depletion age, humankind learned the first aspect of systems; a lesson that John Donne put into the words: 'No man is an island'.

Indeed, no *thing*, man or otherwise, is an island: everything is adjacent in one way or another in the intricate universal topology, related, in a web of relationships, where everything can be connected implicitly or explicitly to every or any other thing in the web. Changes in one portion of the web mean changes in all other portions of the web and once this fundamental rule of systems was learned by Humankind, he was forever more careful with his garbage, especially when it became profitable to do so.

The ceiling occluded and I was cut off, for a time, from the outside.

I am a frail creature, dogged with uncertainty, lacking in personal self-worth at times; but I see that things fit together—click—joyfully like fine machinery, and that understanding is the basis of my morals; for I respect and wish to preserve that fit. It is the reason I believed that longevity was safe with me at the time, for I wouldn't spread it—willy-nilly—throughout Mankind until I had carefully traced out all of the domino chains—

I stopped, thunderstruck. Sheridan had shoved the job of judgment on me as if I were the sole judge, as if the buck could stop with me, and that is not the way things work at all, at all! I admired— marveled at—the man's postures, choice of words, styles of talking, and the way he maneuvered me into the role of an arbitrator, giving me the obligations of a judge—omniscient but detached—when I was intimately woven into the problem. Sheridan knew that, when he forced himself on me and displayed himself as a person loved and respected, I wouldn't have the courage to watch him die. He knew I was particularly sensitive to death. He gambled that I would keep him alive even if I didn't give him the full therapy. He gambled that I would remain in the judge's role long enough for the responsibilities of that august position to cloud my vision; until I would say to myself: 'Why am I keeping this guy on tenterhooks?" and give in. I jumped off the bunk, resolved. Sheridan played a skillful game, a damned skillful game, and he had come perilously close to winning.

But he didn't. And I knew exactly what to do.

I fixed myself an elegant meal with some help from the terminal. Just as I sat down, the compartment bell set up an enormous clatter. Annoyed, I put down my chopsticks, rose, and touched the door plate. My visitor was evidently in a hurry.

"Mr. Fenton, you are to come with me immediately. I—"

I stepped on the brakes gently. "Easy, son. I can't think offhand why I should neglect dinner on your say-so, can you?"

"Mr. Fenton, please, I understand you give security personnel a difficult time as a matter of course, but this is serious. Can you run?"

So we ran. We ran to the slidevator, which then skipped every stop until we reached the sickbay compound. Shortly I was in an emergency care room, and my guess was verified. A young doctor with a stormy look in his eyes confronted me.

"Mr. Fenton? I'm Mr. Sheridan's physician. Mr. Sheridan has had a severe coronary, which at his age—anyway, he wants you here." I peeked past the doctor.

Sheridan wore a mask and had things wired to his chest. His eyes were closed and he was breathing with quick shallow breaths. He looked awful, very old-looking now, frail, the dynamic personality gone. There was a small pick-up on his pillow. His eyes opened a crack, he turned slightly toward us and whispered, "Jim."

"Mr. Sheridan." The doctor turned, businesslike.

"Get lost—clear room of—everyone—but Fenton."

"Mr. Sheridan, I have the responsibility. . . ."

"Jim." The doctor stopped abruptly. I looked at Sheridan. Despite the attack that had beaten his body, despite the tinny speaker and phone amplifier, the voice still carried command.

"Jim—I am a dying—man. Washed up. You—wouldn't deny—a dying man—his last—wish?"

The doctor turned red. Sheridan could still do it, turn a person against himself with a carefully composed sentence. Sheridan was a marvel.

The doctor and nurses and technicians retired behind the door. They were not to return until I allowed them.

Sheridan was peering at me again with that intense predatory look. I looked down at him, waiting.

"Your ... decision, Fenton."

I checked my thoughts. It would be a calculated gamble; chances were there would be unfortunate aspects no matter what the outcome.

"Welcome to the Longevity Club. We're a small and select group."

"What ... What ... " Sheridan seemed almost surprised. Did he have last minute doubts about his game? I tabled the thought.

"All you have to do is relax and give me eye contact. Don't think of anything and when you feel me, *don't resist!*"

I found a chair to sit down on, cradled my head in my hands, and took a stab. I was in. Information flow was very wide and the exchange rate was fast.

"SHERIDAN!"

"Yes ... "

"Don't will anything. Go to sleep."

"The pain ... " I altered the firing threshold of a bundle of synapses.

"What did you do?"

"Later, sleep now. This is not the metamorphosis, this is just to patch you together."

It wasn't the worst session I'd had with death. My fourteenth metamorphosis, the short one, somehow found me in France during the year 1916. I called the shot that World War One wouldn't happen and got drafted in the French infantry. A moment of carelessness found me stitched up the side with a machine-gun burst. I had to keep myself alive *and* metamorphose at the same time. At least Sheridan wasn't halfway sawed through and lying in a trench.

Patchwork kept me busy for about an hour. Sheridan was in relatively healthy shape, so I took the liberty of hyper-regenerating the arterial walls. I worked on the local timing too, so I was sure the heart wouldn't stop on us. With the somatic problems mostly settled and the consequences of a few dozen toppled domino chains cleared up, I woke Sheridan.

"Sheridan."

"Yes."

"How do you feel?"

"Good! Is it over?"

"We haven't even begun. I just rewired you so you can make it through the short haul, which is going to be a rough one. I am going to go through a metamorphosis step by step and you are to take notes. The first thing I'll show you is direct-memory access so you won't forget anything that I show you."

"I could use that trick in a thousand and one ways."

"Now a lot of these processes are traumatic and set up noise in the nervous system. It's painful. I also won't touch the exterior much. That's finishing and I'll leave it to you as practice; besides, it's best not to upset the doctor too much."

"Understandable."

"You ready?"

"Yes."

"This is going to hurt as much as your rubber hose."

I gave Sheridan very practical instruction. If you ever buy a piece of complicated machinery a field representative will come with it. That field representative will give you point-by-point instructions: this knob does this; that lever controls that. He isn't teaching you an overall philosophy, he's telling you how that button sorter can be specifically operated to sort buttons. It's the exact opposite of how I teach control systems and the exact opposite of how I taught That Woman because the two teaching methods stem from entirely different points of view.

Sheridan didn't seem to object.

"It's done."

"That was very comprehensive, Fenton; and this link-up is a very effective method of getting ideas across."

"True, but it's an 'and' link: both of us have to agree to it and either of us can cut at any time." I finished with my voice. "So it's subject to my vagaries."

Sheridan shook his head. The cyanosis was gone, but his exterior, to the quick glance, was about as old as when I first came on board.

Sheridan looked at the clock. "It's been two hours. Gil, let the doctor in; he'll be having kittens."

I opened the door and the doctor was about standing on it with a battalion of security men, it seemed.

"Good Heavens! I was about to break in, Fenton. What . . . ?"

"Are you sure there is anything wrong with Mr. Sheridan? He and I had a good long chat and he doesn't seem the least bit ill," I said innocently. The doctor shoved past me and bee-lined to the telemetry equipment.

"What happened?" he kept on saying through his teeth.

"Security, you're dismissed," Sheridan commanded. "Fenton, if I pull through," with amusement in his eyes, "I'll be in direct contact with you."

Near as I could tell, that ten percent chance was shrinking, and Sheridan would soon be up to his old tricks. I had made my move, however, and only time would tell if I had made the right one.

§ § §

Three days.

I had expected things to happen, but Sheridan was working on a grand scale. The afternoon of the metamorphosis, he had the doctors take him to his personal quarters, where he got out of bed and dismissed them. He relieved his physician and gave him a research post he was after. He then announced that Sheridan Industries would be marketing another First.

Three days. I knew my plan would work, but it might take a week. Meanwhile, Sheridan was going to town.

Sheridan had invited me to the Observatory for a private breakfast. Sheridan had dismissed his personal staff and made his domain 'taboo', while I was forbidden to go into the rest of the Station. I watched the Earth spin silently below my feet. "You've put up with a lot of silliness," I said to her. She bore the comment in silence. I wondered, for the umpteenth time, if my timing was off. A perfectly good scheme shot to Hell by poor timing still loses the war. If my timing was off, could I still patch up the pieces?

Sheridan came strutting down the catwalk. Oh God, I thought for the seventh time that day, Doc Savage and Conan rolled into one.

Sheridan was a magnificent specimen. His skin was bronzed, with muscles rippling smoothly beneath. His hair was blond again and close-cropped. The only real constants his eyes, were still the same—steel grey and penetrating. He tried a mental hook-up, but I had the 'bug-off' shield up. So he shrugged and sat down to a breakfast that was large enough to feed the Golden Horde. Well, he was half of it, anyway. I nursed a cup of coffee—my seventh cup.

"You're bigger than yesterday," I said. "Have you got the inner man represented yet?"

"Yes, I do, and I feel at peace with myself and my exterior, thanks to you." He shot me an engaging, genuine smile. I suspect, knowing his mentality, that Sheridan considered me his only equal; his staff were people with whom words and charm sufficed.

"Don't thank me, you are what you are because . . . well, that's the way you want to be," I said.

"But you taught me how to live and how to do this," said Sheridan, gently flexing his body beautiful. "You pulled me from the grave with your teachings."

"I taught you nothing. You taught yourself. I just told you a few things that you used according to a certain philosophy."

"You're modest, Fenton. That's your only shortcoming: you have no assertive qualities. You neither assert yourself nor impose your ideas on your surroundings. No wonder you've been in the background for a millennium."

"Where would you foreground people be if it wasn't for us background people giving you something to stand out from?"

"True, true—it takes all kinds to make a world. I am going to take advantage of this boon."

"You're going to charge a membership fee to the longevity club."

"More than that, Gil. I am going to make the Sheridan Group the most powerful organization that has ever existed." Sheridan stalked around the room, lecturing me. I finally got around to breakfast, hoping that my timing wasn't off, ready to hear the worst, if it was.

"Nationwide, then worldwide hook-up, right on Day One." Sheridan paced around the room with Terra wheeling beneath his feet. He turned to me.

"Why can't today be Day One?"

"Too soon," I replied around a dripping jam sandwich. "Take it from the authority on longevity. You need a little more practice."

"Hard to believe."

"Besides," I replied, "if you announce today you'll hit the North American continent on Friday. If you wait two days you'll hit 'em on a Monday. There ain't *nothin'* to look forward to on a Monday but another lousy week. The announcement of immortality will break up an otherwise dull day."

"That would be better," Sheridan acquiesced. Turning to an unpowered holographic rig, he said, "People of the nation, I am the director of the Sheridan Group Industries and I have an Important Announcement to make." He smiled and turned back to me. "Sheridan Industries are now offering options on Immortality. You and I will give the first lessons and hire the ones we've processed until we have a good line going. Then you'll be my chief engineer and I'll go back to the management of the Group. The price: no money, just the adoption of The Sheridan Plan; a plan of recommended, rational behavior based on chemotherapy and classroom teaching. It's going to be a wonderful world, Gil."

"Do tell." I chased a bit of egg around. "What about population control?"

"That's in the plan—some special instructions for women," beamed Sheridan. "Having kids will be a privilege."

"I see, always the girl who carries the burden," I observed to Terra, turning slowly in Space.

"Well, there's physical evidence if we catch her. I'm thinking in terms of logistics."

"Or stagnation?" I asked. "How about genetic remixing? How will the gene pool get stirred around?"

"I think Vonner and his boys can handle that; as for senility—well, you know the answer to that one."

"I don't mean senility. What will happen to the culture if the same points of view get banged around century after century?"

"Nor do I see any objection there, Gil; there's no point of view like the right point of view; and that's what The Sheridan Plan is for." He smiled, his hands on his hips. "Next objection! You see I've thought out this entire business of world direction. I am the first scientific ruler this planet has ever had, thanks to you."

Remembered as Sheridan's 'Dr. Frankenstein'? I was horrified.

"We've been over this teaching business," I said. "So what are the logistics of handling everybody and his uncle?"

Sheridan became serious, calculating. "We have to be rather exclusive in our clientele in the first phase. Between you and me, Sheridan is still consolidating its position. We will have to do business with potential investors and world rulers at first, and make the club exclusive, and use the *promise* of longevity to control the masses. As we go along, tying in more rulers and investors, we can consolidate our position and give permission to those populations who are

most in tune with the Sheridan Group." The word 'Industries' had disappeared.

"As near as I can tell," I said musingly, watching the world turn, "we'll have, a century from now, a population with the right point of view, chemically cultivated by the Sheridan Group, which is an instrument of your philosophy." I looked at Sheridan and he nodded. I continued, "People will be born at an insignificant rate, to replace those who were careless with machinery or political points of view. Those born could easily be dealt with early in life, separately, for together they might brew up some silly ideas. Once cultivated, they pose no threat. Most everybody will sit around for millennia on end, nodding to each other, thinking the right kind of thoughts, a worldwide Roman Empire without the boon of the Huns to stir up the show." I again looked at Sheridan. He nodded.

And continued nodding.

Nodding, with a blank stare.

Nodding, with a growing look of horror on his face.

Nodding, he grabbed at what he thought was the table and seized air.

219

Nodding, he shook and stumbled, as neural networks crumbled and revolted.

Nodding, he fell, soaked with sweat, trembling lips trying to form words, with chemical circuits awry, neural circuits oscillating or disengaging, his entire body politic in revolt.

I scratched the back of my head, much relieved. There were a few blows against my bug-off screen, but they weakened, and vanished.

"G-G-G-G-G-G-G—Gil!"

"Nothing I can do about it, chum; you are what you are and that is the bed of roses. Don't complain."

"What's happening? *God,* it hurts!"

"Easy question. You're dying."

"Impossible—I can't reach anything—falling apart. . . . *Help me!* Help the world—"

"I'm helping the world in the most humane way I can; and I guess that means your elimination. Sorry, Sheridan, but I abide by the circumstances of your passing." I folded my hands on the table and watched the heaving, sweating, crawling man.

"You judged me . . . *worthy!*" he growled out. He tried to fix his grey eyes on me but the head kept oscillating about the proper line of sight, giving Sheridan the appearance of nodding yes, no, yes, no.

"Before you pass on, Sheridan, I would like you to know that I almost fell for your judgment game: but I didn't. I never judged you. I did, however, give you an examination, knowing that I could live with the results of the examination, whether you passed or failed."

"Y-y-y-you gave me—*ability!*"

"I didn't know if you truly appreciated the obligations of one who instigates change. Many changes introduced to the culture have had vast side effects, such as the petroleum dirt of our late, great automobile; we lived through that era, you and I. And I, in search of that Universal Why, have come to respect the inter-relatedness of things. I wondered if you had. I knew Terra was a network of dependencies. I also knew you had big plans for it. So after I got out from under that judgment syndrome you offered me, I gave you a microcosm to play with: yourself."

"Long—" Sheridan had stopped trembling now. He drooled.

"No, it wasn't longevity. I showed you a number of system controls that *could* have been used to promote your longevity wish. They could also make you big and handsome overnight. Used with the understanding that the body is an interrelated complex, where introduced changes in themselves trigger related changes, they could make you do a thousand different things. Used without the understanding of the relatedness of things, they kill you. You made yourself big and handsome, pushed your skeleton around, forced growth there, retarded activity here as if your body were one great plaything. Now you die, because you weren't sensitive to the chemical, neural, and electrical systems you bowled over. You kicked over too many domino chains." I looked at him. "And you were on the verge of doing it with Terra. Sheridan, if you can't run yourself right, how the hell do you expect to keep a *planet* straight?"

"You . . . tested me?"

"And you flunked."

Sheridan understood. Before Sheridan shot through, he understood, and died without fear.

And I sat for a long time at the breakfast table, wondering if, philosophies aside, Sheridan was a better man than I for facing fearlessly that which frightens me so. I could have changed him, tweaked a neuron or so while he was asleep to make him a less ambitious man.

But he had called me a man of principles: I didn't approve of his sawbucks, and I didn't approve of his conditioning either. Sheridan died Sheridan.

And at the breakfast table I mourned him for what he could have been.

I finished my sixteenth metamorphosis and attended to Sheridan's rounds. I sent the security force chasing around for a Gilbert Fenton, laid the plans for some very careful dismantling; cancelled an announcement that I had made the previous week, when I was ill and given to curious things. All in all, it was a productive Monday; and I finished out the day, alone, amused at the circumstances that induced me to metamorphose into a very old man.

We learned in the first answer that the proportions of male, female, and bisexual children remain permanently 1:1:1. Because of the decree, every mother has exactly one bisexual child. To preserve the 1:1:1 ratios, the average number of males to a mother must be 1, and the average number of females must also be 1. This makes an average of 3 children per mother.

A